The Lifters

DAVE EGGERS

WITH ILLUSTRATIONS BY

AARON RENIER

A YEARLING BOOK

Text copyright © 2018 by Dave Eggers
Cover art copyright © 2018 by Eric and Terry Fan
Interior illustrations copyright © 2018 by Aaron Renier

All rights reserved. Published in the United States by Yearling,
an imprint of Random House Children's Books, a division of Penguin Random House LLC,
New York. Originally published in hardcover in the United States by Alfred A. Knopf,
an imprint of Random House Children's Books, New York, in 2018.

Yearling and the jumping horse design are registered trademarks of Penguin Random House LLC.

Visit us on the Web! rhcbooks.com

Educators and librarians, for a variety of teaching tools, visit us at RHTeachersLibrarians.com

The Library of Congress has cataloged the hardcover edition of this work as follows:
Names: Eggers, Dave, author. | Renier, Aaron, illustrator.
Title: The lifters / Dave Eggers ; with illustrations by Aaron Renier.
Description: New York : Alfred A. Knopf Books for Young Readers, 2018. |
Summary: Twelve-year-old Gran and his new friend, Catalina, journey underground
to defeat a strange force that threatens their town, Carousel.
Identifiers: LCCN 2018013860 | ISBN 978-1-5247-6416-6 (hardback) |
ISBN 978-1-5247-6417-3 (lib. bdg.) | ISBN 978-1-5247-6418-0 (ebook)
Subjects: | CYAC: Supernatural—Fiction. | Underground areas—Fiction. | Monsters—Fiction. |
Friendship—Fiction. | Moving, Household—Fiction. | BISAC: JUVENILE FICTION / Fantasy &
Magic. | JUVENILE FICTION / Social Issues / Friendship. | JUVENILE FICTION / Monsters.
Classification: LCC PZ7.1.E296 Lif 2018 | DDC [Fic]—dc23

ISBN 978-1-5247-6419-7 (paperback)

Printed in the United States of America
10 9 8 7 6 5 4 3 2 1
First Yearling Edition 2019

Random House Children's Books supports the First Amendment
and celebrates the right to read.

Praise for

The
Lifters

AN INDIE BESTSELLER
A SCHOOL READING LIST (UK) BOOK OF THE MONTH
A JUNIOR LIBRARY GUILD SELECTION

"What to do about the awfulness of the world? You would hope
there was a secret society of clandestine superheroes holding evil at bay.
Dave Eggers's INVENTIVE, GRIPPING *The Lifters* provides something
like that, except it's not superheroes—it's ordinary people, armed with
hockey sticks and bits of an old carousel." —*The Guardian*

"A FAST-PACED yarn of weird business, close calls, and life lessons."
—*San Francisco Chronicle*

"Eggers performs a marvelous sleight of hand, producing a
FIRST-RATE middle grade adventure that doubles as a political
parable for our times." —*The Buffalo News*

"A WARM AND REWARDING read. . . . Eggers skillfully handles the trope
of the kids who save the town, with plenty of humorous adult cluelessness but an
equal measure of compassion." —*The Bulletin of the Center for Children's Books*

"ORIGINAL. . . . Eggers's story moves along briskly thanks
to mounting suspense and bite-size chapters." —*Booklist*

"A WHIMSICAL, FANTASTICAL story with elements of realism. . . .
This atmospheric story's detailed plot moves quickly, and all the characters
experience growth." —*School Library Journal*

"[*The Lifters*] achieves this balance of clean storytelling in short,
sharp chapters with enough EDGE, WIT, AND MYSTERY
to hold a universal appeal." —*The Independent*

"It's the kind of story with a MAGIC that will make you hope and wish you
yourself could just open a door in the hillside." —*The Children's Book Podcast*

"Eggers successfully blends the real and the fantastic in UNEXPECTED ways."
—*Publishers Weekly*

"Dave Eggers's *The Lifters* UNDERSTANDS WHAT IT'S LIKE both inside
and outside the skins of middle-schoolers." —The Center for Fiction

"A MASTERPIECE." —Kidsreads.com

Chapter ONE

Gran did not want to move to Carousel.

Chapter **TWO**

But his parents had little choice.

His father, a mechanic, had not had steady work in many years, for reasons unknown to Gran.

His mother had had an accident when Gran was young, and was now in a wheelchair. His parents never explained quite what happened, and Gran didn't feel right asking. After a while, when people asked Gran about his mother's condition, he just said, "She was born that way." It was the easiest way out of the conversation.

But he remembered when she walked. He remembered that she had once worked as an artist in museums, making the animals in dioramas look realistic. He had a foggy memory of standing, as a

toddler, in an African savannah with her as she touched up the whiskers of a cheetah. That was before the wheelchair.

Then Gran's sister Maisie was born, and his mother hadn't returned to work. Gran's father had built a studio for her, enclosing their deck and filling it with easels and paint and worktables, everything the right height. But Gran couldn't remember her ever using it.

"My art is them now," Gran heard her say to his father one day. At the time, Gran didn't know what that meant.

Something of her talents had rubbed off on Gran. When he was four, his mother began giving him a certain kind of clay, available in hundreds of colors, that hardened when baked in the oven. With this clay, and with his mother's gentle guidance, he formed penguins and dolphins and narwhals—sea creatures who shared the Atlantic with him.

There was a distinct satisfaction in taking a block of blue clay and warming it, rolling it into a ball, then pinching it here to make a fin, squeezing there to make a tail— and suddenly, from a blue ball there was something like a whale. Gran made animals from clay when he was happy, when he was sad, and especially when his parents fought. He was never sure what would happen when his parents argued, how loud it would get or how long it would go on, but he always knew that in twenty minutes, as their voices faded from his mind, he could make a ball of colored clay look like an orca, a manatee, a hammerhead shark.

As he worked, Maisie usually watched. "Doesn't look like anything," she would say as he first rolled the clay.

He would pinch and pull, and she would say, "Looks like a snake. Snakes are boring."

Then he would twist and poke, and something different, and specific, would emerge, and always Maisie acted like it was a miracle.

"How'd you do that?" she would ask, her voice awed. Gran liked nothing better in the world than to hear his sister's voice awed. It gave him immeasurable strength for reasons he could not know.

Chapter **THREE**

B ut over the years, money had grown tighter, and there was nothing left over for clay.

Now work had been offered to Gran's father in Carousel, a town where Gran's great-great-grandparents had once lived.

"Much less expensive there," Gran's father had said.

"Less stressful. Less traffic," Gran's mother had said.

"What about the ocean?" Maisie had said. She was five years old now, and had been amassing a tremendous sand dollar collection.

"There's no ocean there," Gran's mother had said to Maisie and Gran. "But there are hills, and a river winds through the town, and there are trees, and raccoons, and foxes, and more deer than you've ever seen or could count."

Chapter **FOUR**

So one day Gran, his parents, and his sister Maisie left their coastal Atlantic town to drive to Carousel, a hilly hamlet a thousand miles from any sea.

On moving day, Gran's parents did what they did for any long drive: they woke Gran and Maisie up in the middle of the night, carried them to the car, buckled them in, stuffed pillows under the seat belts, and covered them with blankets.

"I am a burrito!" Maisie said.

"You are not a burrito," her father said. "Go back to sleep."

When Gran and Maisie next woke up, they were at a gas station. "Halfway there," their mother said. It was warm in the car, so they fell asleep again. The next time they woke, they were parked

7

in front of a narrow two-story house located midway up a slope crowded with other wooden homes.

"This is Carousel," their mother said.

"This is our new house," their father said. "Not that it's new. My great-grandfather built it."

"When?" Gran asked.

His father opened the car's passenger side door and sat, putting on his boots. (He liked to drive barefoot.) He paused for a long moment, his right boot in his left hand. "Shoot. Now I can't remember. I know it's on a plaque inside. Or used to be. I want to say it was 1924. Or 1942. I'm almost sure it was an even number."

"Why's the house crooked?" Maisie said.

"Maisie, shush," her mother said.

They got out of the car and stood for a moment on the sidewalk, which zigzagged up and down the hill, in front of the other homes that dotted the street. Gran agreed with Maisie: the house looked crooked. The first floor seemed to be leaning to the right, and the second floor leaned to the left, and all of it seemed to be leaning ever so slightly downhill. But Gran knew saying any of this might hurt his father's feelings, so he stayed quiet.

Gran's father was standing with his hands on his hips, his head tilted and eyes squinting at the house, as if trying to figure it out.

"Something's off," his father said.

"It's fine, Ben," his mother said. "It's just fine."

Chapter **FIVE**

This new house and this new town were in every way different from where Gran's family had come. Their previous home was an apartment near the sea, and there, the landscape of their town had been flat, and most of it paved. The only time Gran had seen any kind of distance was when he went to the beach, where he could see the wide sweep of the coast.

But Carousel was hilly and wild. The roads were curvy and full of potholes. There were barns next to gravel mountains next to auto parts stores next to wide-open pastures.

In their apartment by the sea, the doors had never made a sound, but the front door of this house in Carousel creaked like an old man waking from a thousand-year slumber.

"I'll fix that," Gran's father said.

When Gran's father showed Gran the bedroom he'd be sharing with Maisie, he couldn't believe what he saw out of his window. He'd never seen views like this. He could see most of the town below, and the river that separated the town from a steep expanse of wooded hills beyond. He could see the railroad that ran along the silver zigzag river, and could see the steeples of the two churches, and could see people coming and going into the grocery twenty blocks away. Next to the grocery store was some kind of flea market, and just up from that was a red brick building that Gran assumed was City Hall.

"Come up here!" his father yelled.

Gran looked into the hallway, where he saw a ladder leading up.

"We have an attic, Gran!" his father said from above. Now Maisie appeared on the second-floor landing.

Gran and Maisie had never seen an attic before. Apartments don't usually have attics.

Gran climbed the ladder and Maisie followed, but when she got to the top of the ladder, she didn't want to go farther. She scurried quickly back down.

"Too dark," she said.

It was indeed dark, and smelled like warm wood. Gran made his way to his father, who knelt over an old cardboard box.

"My great-grandfather's stuff, I'm guessing," he said.

Gran peered in. It was a mess of old tools and scraps of metal. There were dark metal fragments of a dozen shapes and tools that

neither Gran nor his father had ever seen before. There was a giant C, about the size of Gran's hand, that he picked up. It was etched with beautiful lines that entwined like the paths of birds.

"That's a nice one. Brass. I think he was a blacksmith," Gran's father said. "But I had no idea he'd kept all this stuff."

"What are you going to do with it all?" Gran asked.

"No idea," Gran's father said.

Chapter **SIX**

G ran arrived well after the school year had begun, which is not an easy time to arrive in any new place. But he was optimistic. For one thing, he looked forward to trying out his new name.

Gran had never been Gran before. He had been born with the name Granite. His father had insisted on giving him a sturdy first name to compensate for his last name, which was Flowerpetal.

"We needed to balance it out a bit," his father had explained. "We couldn't name you Blossom, right?"

But the name Granite came with its own problems. Gran had to explain it to everyone he met. He usually had to spell it. If his name had been Michael or Derrick, there would be no need to pause, explain, to spell or discuss the nature of names, of unusual names, or how you got them. He would not have to talk about earth science, the properties of granite as opposed to marble or sandstone. He just wanted a name that was a name—easily understood, easily spelled.

So when his family moved to Carousel, Granite decided to shorten his name to Gran. Gran almost sounded like *Grand*, which was a good thing, and no one would ask how to spell Gran. If someone didn't know how to spell Gran, they wouldn't admit it. Gran was convinced that this easy change would solve all his name-related problems.

But he was only partially correct.

Chapter **SEVEN**

Carousel Middle School was only half a mile away, and Gran could get there by walking up the hill, and then over, and then up a ways, and then over, then up a ways one last time.

, "And Maisie's school is on the way," Gran's mother said the first day, which wasn't the first day at all. The rest of Maisie's classmates had been in school for three weeks. Gran's school had been in session for four.

Gran and Maisie set out on a warm morning in mid-September and were happy to be able to walk to school. All their lives they'd been driven to school, picked up from school and driven to stores and playdates, but this, simply leaving the house and walking on their own—it made this new situation easier to accept.

"Should we run?" Maisie asked when they left the house.

They ran up the hill, but it was so steep they were quickly tired. They stopped in front of an extremely narrow house on the corner. It was painted burgundy, and had a turret rising from its roof like a torch.

"Who's that man?" Maisie asked.

There was a sign on the narrow home's scrubby lawn, and on the sign, a word bubble extended from the mouth of a bald man with a bushy mustache. "No on Propositions P&S! Yes on Propositions M&H!" he appeared to be yelling. The sign indicated that the man's name was Dr. Walter Woolford.

"He looks like a gopher," Maisie said.

Gran told her it wasn't polite to compare adults to rodents, but secretly he knew that Maisie was right. This man named Dr. Walter Woolford did look a lot like a gopher, with the same oversized cheeks and protruding front teeth.

Gran read the words on the sign to Maisie, but he didn't know how to explain who Dr. Walter Woolford was, or anything about Propositions P&S or M&H.

"Look," Maisie said.

On the other side of the same lawn, there was a different sign. This one featured a kindly-looking woman who reminded Gran of pictures of his own grandmother, his mother's mother. Both his grandmother and this woman had long white hair tied in a ponytail and dark, smiling eyes. This woman's name was Phyllis Feeley, and her advice was YES ON PROPOSITIONS P&S! NO ON PROPOSITIONS M&H!

Gran wondered what Propositions P&S were, what Propositions M&H were, and how it could be that the people on the signs could

be disagreeing with each other so vehemently on the same lawn. While he was wondering all this, a screeching voice came from the burgundy home. "Loiterer!" the voice yelled. "Off the grass!"

It was the voice of a middle-aged woman, and Gran located its source: a silhouette standing in the window of the narrow house.

"Is she yelling at us?" Maisie asked.

Gran was sure she couldn't be. He was twelve years old and had never been yelled at by a stranger.

"Leave them alone, Theresa," said another voice, this one soothing, like warm water bubbling from a kettle. Gran saw a different woman's silhouette in the window of the other side of the same house. "They're only kids!"

"Quiet, Therése!" the first woman screeched.

Now Gran had the feeling they were talking about him and Maisie. He took Maisie's hand and they slowly backed away from the lawn until they were safely on the sidewalk.

"Now move along!" said the screechy silhouette. "Or I'll send the dog out."

"Let them be," said the warm-water woman. "And your dog wouldn't scare anyone anyway. He weighs less than a loaf of bread."

Gran and Maisie moved briskly along the sidewalk, and as they did, Gran caught a glimpse of two separate doghouses, nearly identical, on either side of the narrow burgundy house. In each doghouse there was the tiny face of a tiny dog—they seemed to be twins—and both seemed bored beyond tears by the bickering of the women in the windows.

The back and forth continued between the two voices until Gran and Maisie were long gone.

Chapter **EIGHT**

As soon as they saw the playground of Carousel Elementary, Maisie ran to it as if she'd been going there all year.

"Wait," Gran said, but she had already disappeared into a winding, zebra-striped tube. Only her feet were visible.

Gran found Maisie's teacher, a young woman with a heart-shaped face and bronze skin. "That's my sister," he told her. "The one going the wrong way on the slide."

"I noticed someone new," the teacher said. "It's been years since we had a new family in town. She must be Maisie. And you are?"

"Gran," Gran said. He was instantly soaked in sweat. He'd never tried his new name before.

"Gran?" the teacher repeated.

"Yes," he said. He waited with dread to see how the heart-faced teacher would react, but she simply said "Got it" before turning her attention back to the playground.

Gran walked on, feeling reasonably good about how that had gone, and soon saw an unusual man. Across the street and going his way, there was a grown man riding a child's dirtbike. The man was wearing a tanktop, shorts, long black socks and bright orange sneakers. His legs and arms were covered with blue tattoos, and following him sullenly was a pitbull the color of mud.

"Sup," he said to Gran.

Gran had never seen a grown man on a child's dirtbike before. The men where Gran used to live usually wore suits, or at least dress shirts, and he rarely saw them out and about like this in the middle of the morning; usually they were at work. Gran was thinking about this man, and about the town, when he saw his new school.

Chapter **NINE**

Carousel Middle School was very old and sat atop a ridge that seemed to be falling away beneath it. The building had been made of gray and purple and pink bricks that alternated as if the bricklayers hadn't been able to gather enough of any one color, or couldn't decide on any logical pattern. The whole building leaned heavily toward the downward slope below, giving the impression it would fall at any provocation.

Gran entered the building, and nothing happened. That is, this is not a story where the schoolmates of the protagonist are cruel to him. This is a story where the classmates ignore the protagonist altogether. But there didn't seem to be any reason why. At first, when Gran entered the school and made his way around the hallways and

through his first few classes, he figured it was because he was small.

Gran had never been especially small before. In his previous school, he was average-sized. But now, in Carousel, Gran felt like he'd shrunk. Sometime between when he'd left his old school and arrived at this one, either he'd shrunk five inches or everyone else had grown that much. He was now the shortest boy in his class, and probably the skinniest, too.

But no one said anything about this. No one called him any names. In class, when they passed papers back to him, they said nothing. When he asked where the bathroom was, they only pointed. When he bumped into a large boy whose baby-blue shirt was far too small—it looked more like a bib—that boy said nothing at all. He brushed Gran away as he would a spiderweb.

Even the teachers barely addressed him. They spoke to the classes generally, but when the bell rang to announce school was out, Gran was absolutely sure no one had said his name all day.

Chapter **TEN**

"**H**ow was school?" his mother asked.

Though she was in a wheelchair, her legs withered and arranged in a tight double S, Gran's mother seemed to be everywhere at once, moving around the first floor of the new house with great speed.

"I am definitely the queen of school," Maisie announced, and pretended to jump rope, without a rope.

Gran told his mother that his school was fine, and told her, also, that no one had said anything to him all day.

"Stop that, Maisie," Gran's mother said, and wheeled herself over to him. She tilted her head sympathetically and, at a loss for words, she simply pulled him onto her lap. Tired and confused, he allowed it. Maisie went back to jumping rope without a rope.

When Gran's father came home from work, he looked tired and confused, too. He usually spent five minutes at the sink, washing the grease from his hands, but this time went straight for the living room. "Hello, my loves," he said, and sat heavily down on the couch. Maisie climbed onto his lap and he wrapped his arms around her. His hands were still clean.

Gran's father turned Maisie around so she faced out, toward Gran and his mother, then he moved Maisie's arms and legs as if she were dancing. He pumped her arms up and down, kicked her legs out like she was a marionette. Watching the two of them, Gran could forget his father was there, controlling her, and for a moment it looked like his five-year-old sister was an expert dancer, her limbs flying around like a showgirl's. Gran laughed, his mother laughed, and Maisie screamed with joy for a full minute.

Then she threw up.

Chapter **ELEVEN**

Maisie threw up more than the average person. More so, certainly, than anyone else in the Flowerpetal family. She threw up in cars, and on swings, and always when Gran's father tossed her around. But still she loved to be lifted and swung; the throwing up was just part of it, the part where it was time to stop playing and clean up.

"I'll get the mop," Gran said.

The Flowerpetals always did something unusual when it was time to clean up. They did it together. Gran couldn't place when this started, but as far back as he could remember, they had been cleaning up Maisie's vomit together. The job got done faster that way, and was actually kind of fun.

"What do I see here?" Gran's father said, examining the pink-and-green puddle on the floor. "Looks like spinach. And pears. And gummy bears. Wait, did I just write a poem?"

They all laughed, and the job was done in minutes. All that was left was to open the windows and light a candle. Maisie always opened the window. Gran's mother usually lit the candle. Gran's job was to take the garbage, now containing Maisie's latest output, outside.

"First vomit in the new house," Gran's father said when Gran returned.

"Now it's officially a home," Gran's mother said.

Maisie loved the attention. She wasn't embarrassed at all.

When the Flowerpetals had lived near the ocean, their apartment had four rooms—the living room, the kitchen (which really was just an extension of the living room), the bathroom, and the bedroom, which they all shared.

And because the apartment was small, they had all participated in just about everything happening inside. If Gran's mother or father was cooking, they all helped in some way. If someone started cleaning the apartment, everyone joined in. It was hard to avoid—there was nowhere to hide.

This new house, with two stories and seven rooms, was cavernous by comparison. But there was still work to do. Gran's father had begun building a ramp for Gran's mother, from the front door to the driveway. The incline was not so bad as it was—she could manage—but he wanted it to be easier. There was also the matter of the sinks and the counters. They had to be lowered. And then the cabinets underneath had to be removed—otherwise Gran's mother had nowhere to put her legs.

"Let's start with the bathroom," he said.

Chapter **TWELVE**

But there is a sadness that courses through a house where money is uncertain. From the bedroom he shared with his sister, after she was asleep, all that first week and the next, Gran would hear his parents talk quietly about money.

His father did not have a job like some jobs—where an adult is paid a salary, steadily, dependably. Instead, Gran's father was paid each afternoon for the work he did that day, and was not sure whether or not he would get work the next.

From what Gran could gather, his father had been told that Carousel needed a mechanic, but when they arrived—after moving a thousand miles—he was told the local auto shop didn't have much work after all. People were giving up their cars and trucks. Gran remembered seeing the grown man riding a boy's dirtbike. There wasn't enough money in the town to pay for repairs to old vehicles, let alone buy new ones.

When Gran's father did not get work, he was at home when Gran got home from school, and the nights were long. His parents' murmuring sometimes turned to hissing, and sometimes fell to yelling.

On days when their voices became loud, Gran would look to Maisie, sleeping across from him, and wonder if she could hear what he heard. She never did wake up, but she turned left and right and kicked the covers from her, as if wanting to get free.

Then, one morning, Gran's father's car was gone.

"He went looking for work," his mother said. "He heard about something a few hundred miles south."

"So why are we here?" Maisie asked.

"He'll be back this weekend," Gran's mother said. "Get your jackets on. It's supposed to be colder today."

Chapter **THIRTEEN**

Every morning, Gran and Maisie walked up the hill, past the burgundy house, where they heard the two women arguing over the issues presented on their lawn signs. Gran and Maisie walked past the twin dogs and their exasperation with the bickering, past Dr. Walter Woolford, who was against Propositions P&S and for Propositions M&H, and past Phyllis Feeley, who was for Propositions P&S and against Propositions M&H. Every day Gran saw the same man riding the dirtbike, followed by the same sullen pitbull whose fur was the color of mud.

Gran would drop off Maisie at her elementary school and continue on to his own school, the purple-and-gray one slanting from the ridge, where no one knew his name.

Or rather, they knew but did not care.

It was the Monday of his third week when his name was first spoken by a teacher. Until then, they had preferred not to do roll call, so Gran had simply shown up, and because he never raised his hand in class, he was never called on, and his name was never uttered. Until this certain Monday three weeks in. It was then that Ms. Rhapsod, his homeroom teacher, made an announcement.

"It's come to my attention that some of you have nicknames you'd like to use," she said. "Greta Rose Nagel informed me today that she wants to be called Greta R-N, for example. So if there's anyone else who wishes to amend or shorten their name, let me know. I'm not especially patient when it comes to such things. Once I put your nickname or whatever it is down on this attendance form, that will be it, period. I'll send the change to all your other teachers and that will be that. No going back."

This was the moment that Gran had been waiting for, but it was very different than what he'd envisioned. He hadn't expected it to be so public and so final.

"Anna Applegate?" Ms. Rhapsod said. "No change?"

Anna shook her head.

"Nathan Delacroix?" she said. "You want to be Nat or Nathan-D? Something like that?"

"No thanks," Nathan said.

Gran knew his name was coming up. Flowerpetal was dangerously close to Delacroix. And even closer to Esterhaus and Estrada. His shoulders tensed as those students' names were called.

"Granite Flowerpetal?" Ms. Rhapsod said. Saying his name, her neck snapped back as if she'd just smelled something rotten. There were a few snickers and scoffs.

"Stop," she said, and the snickering and scoffing ended. She looked at Gran as if seeing him for the first time. "Where'd you come from? Have you been in this class all year?"

"Yes sir. I mean, ma'am," Gran said. "I mean, most of it."

For a moment she seemed almost apologetic. Then she returned to her businesslike manner. "Name change for you, Granite Flowerpetal?"

Gran's skin burned and his heart rattled.

"Back at my old school they called me Gran," he managed.

"Okay, Gran it is," Ms. Rhapsod said, and made a note on her attendance sheet.

Chapter **FOURTEEN**

After the nickname session, no one had said anything to Gran for the rest of the period. In the hallway after class, no one made jokes, no one seemed to be gossiping about him. The bell rang, and when he sat down for his first-period class, he seemed again to be invisible. A state of being which, for the time being, he welcomed.

It wasn't until midway through the second period, health class, that he found the note in his textbook. It was on a standard piece of notebook paper, folded in half. The handwriting was small and precise and rendered in black. He was no handwriting expert, but he knew that most of the boys in his class had crazed and jagged handwriting, while the girls' writing was loopy and precise. This note was of the second variety.

Dear Granite/Gran,

I understand why you'd want to change your name from Granite. But why change it to Gran? Don't you realize Gran sounds like you're a grandmother? A twelve-year-old boy shouldn't be called the same thing I call my grandmother. Which is Gran.

Question of the day: Why didn't you just change your name to Grant? That's a real name.

Signed,

Your classmate.

Gran's face tingled. His stomach tied itself into braids. He looked around, suddenly sure that the writer of the note was close by, watching him.

But no one was looking at him.

He turned back to the note, read it again, and knew it was cor-

rect. He hadn't thought of the best solution to the problem. Grant. Of course. Grant would have worked far better than Gran. And now he had to live with Gran in every class, the rest of the year.

There would be more snickering. More scoffing. Probably some pointing, staring, laughing and ridicule.

Chapter **FIFTEEN**

But none of that happened.

No one said anything the rest of that day. The next day, Ms. Rhapsod went back to her usual way of not calling attendance, and the rest of the teachers, who never called attendance in the first place, continued in their usual way.

Even the students who had snickered and scoffed the first time they heard the name Granite Flowerpetal seemed to have forgotten about Gran's full name, and his nickname, too. They never scoffed again. They never snickered. In fact, they never noticed him. Never looked at him.

No one did.

No one spoke to him.

Which led Gran to wonder if he was, in fact, real.

How can a person be real when four hundred and twelve other people, his fellow students, could not see him?

The days went on, and finally Gran, at the end of his first month in Carousel, walked out of the school and into the bright morning, and was so overcome with the idea that he might not be real that he thought he might be able to walk through walls.

How could he be sure he couldn't walk through a wall? He had never tried it. So he walked around the side of the school, to a spot where he thought he was alone and unseen. Then he squared his shoulders and walked three quick steady steps toward the building. When most people would have stopped, he continued.

Chapter **SIXTEEN**

The pain of bricks against one's head cannot be overstated. Given that bricks are quite solid, walking into them truly hurts. Anyone who has walked into a structure made of this material—bricks—will tell you this.

Gran was on the ground, holding his head, feeling the slippery blood on his hands, when he heard a voice.

"You just walked into a building."

It was a girl's voice. Gran lifted his head, and through his blood-matted hair he saw that it was a dark-eyed girl from his third-period history class. He remembered her because, next to him, she was the shortest person in the class, just a hair taller than Gran. And every day she wore the same thing: heavy brown boots, usually dirty, jeans, a T-shirt—always bearing the face of an older woman with glasses and her hair in a bun—and a flannel shirt tied around her waist. Gran had wondered who the old woman on her shirt was; she looked familiar. But he did know who the girl wearing this shirt was.

Her name was Catalina.

Catalina Catalan.

Chapter **SEVENTEEN**

"**H**ere," she said, and dabbed at the blood with a cloth.

When Gran could see clearly again, he saw that the cloth was a shirt, the flannel shirt she usually wore around her waist.

"Thanks," Gran said. "Sorry about your shirt."

"It's fine," she said. "I turned it inside out first. The blood will be on the inside, where it belongs, right?"

Gran didn't know what to say.

"You're Gran, right?" she said. "You got my note?"

It took Gran a second to connect this actual person in front of him with the anonymous note he'd received. His stomach collapsed like an accordion.

"Were you looking for a door?" she asked.

The note had been unkind, but here she was, talking to him, which seemed a brand of kindness. He decided he preferred this, talking to someone who had judged him cruelly, to not talking to anyone at all.

"No, I . . ." He knew he couldn't explain it without seeming insane. "I'm new here," he said, hoping that might explain it all.

"That explains nothing," she said, and stood. Then she made a huffing sort of sound that seemed to mean she was ready to leave.

"Get up," Catalina said, and held out her hand.

Gran took her hand and she lifted him up with surprising strength. Also surprising was that Catalina's hand didn't feel like any girl's hand that he'd ever known—not that he had much experience touching the hands of girls his age. Catalina's hand was rough and callused. It felt to Gran like shaking his father's hand.

"Try not to walk into any more walls, Granny," she said, then turned, tied the shirt around her waist again, and walked off.

Chapter **EIGHTEEN**

It goes without saying that after this incident, Catalina Catalan became very interesting to Gran. He thought about her throughout the rest of the school day. He thought about her during health class, as the teacher, a short, muscle-bound man named Mr. Cage, enumerated the ways students could get and transmit lice. He thought about her during science class, as Ms. Zywicki passed around a furry gray mass, enclosed in a clear plastic box, that she said was the scat of an Indonesian leopard. As fascinating as lice and feces were to Gran, they were crowded out by thoughts of Catalina Catalan.

The human mind is a passionate thing. It flings itself toward new things, new people, and it can quickly lose

track of everything else. Thus Catalina overtook Gran's mind. He thought about her dark eyes, her dark hair, her strength as she helped him up. But more than any of that he thought how strange and good it was to hear someone, another person his age, speak to him at all.

Chapter **NINETEEN**

When school let out, Gran rushed outside. His plan was to install himself on the front steps, hoping to see Catalina on her way out. Beyond that, he had nothing in mind.

And so he stood like a stone as four hundred students passed around him like water, watching carefully for Catalina Catalan, who he was sure he could not miss.

But he did miss her.

When almost everyone had left the school and the human river had become a trickle, he turned around and saw Catalina Catalan in the distance. She'd somehow walked out the front door and had passed him without his noticing. And she was moving with incredible speed.

Gran, though, could not move with incredible speed. After the first few weeks of school, his workload had become so great that he had been bringing his books to and from school in a rollerbag. This was normally fine and good, but was not fine and good today, because the rollerbag slowed him down ridiculously, and Catalina was ridiculously quick.

She was ridiculously quick in part because she was not pulling a rollerbag. This allowed her to almost fly across the street and down the grassy hill beyond.

Still, Gran hurried down the steps, his rollerbag jerking and tumbling after him. He crossed the street and then stopped on the other side, looking down the hill.

He saw her, walking under the dappled light of a birch forest below. Her hair was black and had a high sheen to it, something like obsidian, and because she walked in a certain way, bouncing high on the balls of her feet, he could easily pick her out. Gran hurried down the grassy hill as she disappeared into the denser woods beyond.

Gran's rollerbag was heavy and unwieldy, twisting and grinding as he ran, and he thought of leaving it somewhere so he could run quicker. But he knew that if he came home without it, or if he lost anything inside it, his parents would be devastated. Or his mother would be. She used this word sometimes when she was disappointed in him. "I'm devastated, Gran," she would say, and he couldn't bear it.

So he kept the rollerbag, and he wound through the trees, catching no sign of Catalina Catalan, until finally, when the trees opened up to reveal a narrow valley, he saw her. In fact, he saw her too clearly, and now that there were no trees to hide him, he knew if she turned around she would see him, unhidden. What would she think? She would wonder why the kid who walked into walls was now running after her, sweating and pulling a forty-pound rollerbag.

But she didn't turn around.

There was a wind swirling through the valley, and it was unlikely she could hear him. She was walking quickly, determinedly, and she seemed to have no worries about who might be following her.

The path she followed wound through the valley and then disappeared around a bend. When she, too, disappeared around this bend, he took off, covering as much ground as he could, as fast as he could.

When he came around the bend, there was no sign of Catalina Catalan. The path unspooled for a half mile at least, unobstructed. If she was still on the path, he would have seen her. In fact, there was open hillside all around. Not a tree in sight. Nothing, not even a gerbil, could hide there.

So where had she gone?

Chapter **TWENTY**

The next day, a Friday, Catalina Catalan wasn't at school.

Between classes, Gran looked for her everywhere. She wasn't in homeroom and she wasn't in third period. She was nowhere. He knew it was normal enough to be absent one day, but Gran found his thoughts drifting to troubling places. What if something had happened to her in the valley the day before? He pored over a mental picture of a great condor swooping down, taking her away. How else could someone disappear the way she did?

During the lunch-and-recess period, forty minutes where the students ate their lunches as quickly as possible and fled the building for the school's lawn and playground, Gran took his paper bag with him, intending to spend the time looking for Catalina. He wouldn't miss the loud cafeteria, and he wouldn't miss the game the boys played after eating. It was a strange game. About twenty of them would stand in a circle, and then would take turns running at each other. When the runner got close to the opposite edge of the circle, he would leap at whoever was standing there and try to kick them in the chest. Crucial to the game was that the standing boy couldn't move. He had to take the kick straight on.

"All right!" the boys would yell after contact was made.

Maybe not, Gran had thought when he first saw the game in action. So every lunch-and-recess period, he'd found different things to do—most of them involving settling into the most out-of-the-way place he could so he could eat unnoticed.

Now, with Catalina missing, he had not just the motive to stay away from the playground, but a mission. So he explored parts of the school he'd never ventured to, in the irrational hope of finding her in some secret corner of the campus. Maybe, he thought, she'd changed classes, or changed grades? Maybe she'd been bumped up to junior high? She was smart, so couldn't that be a possibility?

Gran brought his lunch with him as he went to the wing of the school where the arts classrooms were.

Closed said a sign on the door of the visual arts room.

Fin said the sign on the door of the theater arts room.

Discontinued for Now read the sign on the music room door.

Beneath it, someone had taped one of the Yes on Propositions P&S signs Gran had been seeing on his way to school.

At the end of the hall, a set of steps led to the basement. Gran tried every door, finding them all locked, until one doorknob turned. He pushed the door open and walked in tentatively.

"Hello?" he said.

Inside he found what seemed to be a storage space for just about everything the school wasn't using at the moment. Desks were stacked six high, flanked by looming towers of wooden chairs. There were empty aquariums, papier-mâché buffalos, football helmets and orange traffic cones. There were track hurdles and unicycles and hockey sticks, and behind those, there were old computers and printers and podiums, and behind those, there was a mountain of enormous half-deflated balls Gran remembered from his old school. When inflated, they were huge, bigger than him. Earth balls, his phys ed teacher had called them.

Closer to the door, there was something like an office. Whoever managed this space worked here too. There was a cluttered desk, and all around it, at least a dozen rusted and mismatched file cabinets. They stood like a wall of skyscrapers across from an old leather couch strewn with books.

On the wall above the couch there were pictures of horses, and horse races, and medals, and ribbons. Whoever decorated the room, Gran thought, had a thing for horses.

"Do we have an appointment?" a man's voice boomed from behind Gran. Gran had been so engrossed in the photos that he hadn't heard the entrance of a man who now stood next to him.

"Sorry," Gran said, and moved toward the door.

"Relax. I was kidding," the man said. "Who sent you and what do they need?"

The man, who seemed to be grandparent age, was exceptionally small for a grown person. He was only a few inches taller than Gran, and didn't seem to be much heavier. He had a faint accent, too, but Gran couldn't place it.

"I'm not . . . No one sent me," Gran managed to say. He was so ashamed of having snuck into the room uninvited that he wanted only to leave.

"Sit down," the man said. "Usually it's one of the gym teachers who sends kids down to get an extra ball or a hula hoop from me. You just wandered in, eh?"

"I was looking for someone. I didn't mean to . . ."

"Really. Relax. It's okay. You didn't feel like standing in a circle, getting kicked?" He laughed inclusively, hoping Gran would join in, but Gran was still too nervous to find anything amusing.

"No problem. No problem," the man said. He nodded at Gran's lunch. "Eat if you want. I eat here, too. See?" He walked over to one of the filing cabinets, opened it, and removed an enormous submarine sandwich, easily as big as his head. He sat down on a metal chair facing Gran, unwrapped his sandwich and took an enormous bite. "Door was unlocked?" he asked with his mouth full.

Gran nodded, and thought about opening his lunch and eating, too. He was hungry, but still thought it would be easier just to leave.

"I usually lock the door," the man said. With all the food in his mouth, it sounded like he was talking through a pillow. "You have a name?"

"Gran," Gran said.

The man smiled. "Grande? I like that. That's a strong name. It means 'big' en español. You know this?"

"No, it's Gran . . . t." Gran wasn't sure why he added a *t* this time, but he did—though it was the quietest of *t*'s at the end, like a tiny tail at the end of a giant dog.

"Grant?" the man said. He repeated the name exactly as Gran had said it. There was something so respectful about the way he did this that Gran couldn't correct him.

"It's short for Granite. Like the rock," Gran said.

The man took a long look at Gran, then took another crack at his sandwich and chewed contentedly. In the few minutes since he'd sat down, he managed to devour most of a foot-long ham and cheese.

"Well, Grant, I am El Duque," he said, his mouth full again. "You know any Spanish? It means 'the Duke.'" He pointed to a flag, red, blue and white, on the wall behind him that had the words *The Duke* and *El Duque* embroidered on it. "That was from my riding days. I was a jockey. You ever ride a horse?"

"Not a real one," Gran said. "Maybe once on a merry-go-round." He didn't want this man to think he was still riding on merry-go-rounds, so he added, "When I was a kid."

A thunderous laugh shook the room. It had come from the Duke. Though he was very small, his laugh was enormous. When he was finished, he took another bite of his sandwich and pointed the rest of it at Gran.

"When you were a kid. Right. So you just came in here to eat," he said, and let out a quick grunt, as if he'd figured it all out and it made perfect sense.

There was a knock on the door.

"Yes?" the Duke said.

The door cracked open and a head appeared. It looked a lot like the head of Ms. Rhapsod, one of Gran's teachers.

"No more desks," the Duke said.

"But—" the head said. It sounded like Ms. Rhapsod, too.

"No desks," the Duke said. "No bookshelves. No projection screens. No aquariums."

"But where—?"

"Don't know. Don't care. No more room," the Duke said.

The head disappeared.

The Duke turned back to Gran, smiled and rolled his eyes, as if he had to apologize to his guest for a noisy neighbor. "I usually just sit here and listen to music during lunch," he said. "You like Cuban music?"

Gran wasn't sure if he'd ever heard Cuban music. The Duke walked over to another file cabinet and opened a low drawer, revealing a small turntable. He turned a knob, which set the record spinning. He dropped the needle. The music was tinny and not very loud, but the Duke closed his eyes as if he were hearing the greatest band play his favorite song at full volume.

The Duke pointed at Gran. "Ah, I think you like it. I see your shoulders moving. Look at Grant go!"

Gran hadn't realized his shoulders were moving at all, but he didn't argue with the Duke. The music was catchy, and Gran deduced that maybe this is where the Duke had come from: Cuba. He had a faint recollection that they spoke Spanish in Cuba.

"Listen, listen," the Duke said, pointing to the record player. His eyes closed, and his hand conducted in the air to a certain progression of notes and words he liked. When he opened his eyes, he smiled at Gran.

"You're fun, Grant," the Duke said. "You should come again sometime. Keep me company. I'll bring more records I think you'll like. Eat up, though. You only have ten minutes till the next period. I'll play another song."

The Duke went to the filing cabinet for a new record, and when he dropped the needle to the vinyl, Gran opened his lunch.

Chapter **TWENTY-ONE**

When Gran went to bed on Friday, his father was not home. On Saturday morning, he was on the couch.

"Drove all night," he said. His hands, dirty again, were raised over his head, as if in surrender. The work he'd found that week, he said, was five hundred miles away. "Got home at four in the morning."

Maisie climbed onto his chest and perched herself regally. "Meow," she said, and began to groom herself as a cat would.

"You're getting good at that," Gran's father noted.

Gran's father barely moved all that day. He napped on the couch in the morning and afternoon, and in between, he sat up so he and

Gran's mother could pore over bills and murmur to each other, occasionally reshuffling the bills into a different order.

That night, from their bedroom there was more urgent whispering. A few loud words escaped.

On Sunday afternoon he was gone again.

Chapter **TWENTY-TWO**

O n Monday, Catalina Catalan was back at school.

It had been four days since Gran had seen her, and when he spotted her across the school's main hallway, at first he couldn't quite believe it. He stood in the middle of the hall and stared. She was wearing what she usually wore, a T-shirt bearing the face of an older woman with glasses and her hair in a bun, and again a flannel shirt was tied around her waist. Its sleeves dangled around her jeans, worn over dirty brown boots.

The bell rang, telling them they had one minute left to get to class, but he didn't move until she moved, until she'd walked the opposite way and slipped into her classroom. She hadn't seen him.

With a heavy sigh, he turned and made his way to his first class, math, taught by an impossibly tall man named Mr. Plain.

The next class they had together was third period, and he hoped that somehow he could conjure the courage to speak to her. He wanted to ask her where she'd gone on Thursday afternoon, how she'd disappeared. But when he entered the classroom, she wasn't there. As the students filed in and the bell marking the beginning of class rang, she was nowhere to be found.

His seat was at the front, and as he thought about the implications of this, that she was again absent, he heard the back door of the classroom open. He turned and there she was. The teacher, Ms. Hamid, was not amused. Ms. Hamid was fond of purples and pinks in her clothing, but her attitude was not so flowery. She was stern and businesslike, and she set her words down carefully, each word clicking into place, as if she were assembling a puzzle made of glass.

"Miss Catalan," Ms. Hamid said, "I assume you know that a yawning chasm of time had lapsed between when the bell rang and when you arrived."

"Yes I do."

"And I assume you know the procedure that ensues after such a yawning chasm of time?"

"Yes."

"Good. Then be on your way. Return with a yellow slip."

And Catalina picked up her books and was gone.

Gran was vaguely aware that if a student was late for class, that student had to go to the office, get a yellow slip acknowledging his or her tardiness, and then return to the class. It all seemed strange, given that during all this, the offender missed another fifteen minutes of class time, but it was the way of the school.

The strange thing in this case, stranger than the yellow-slip procedure, was that Catalina Catalan did not return after fifteen minutes. She didn't return at all.

Chapter **TWENTY-THREE**

When Gran got home that evening, just in time to help with dinner, he found his mother looking out the window and his sister Maisie pretending to be a cat.

"Meow," she said to him.

His mother made no sound. This was the first time he could remember her not greeting him when he got home.

"Oh," she said, finally.

Gran began setting the table.

"Just us three tonight," his mother said. She explained that Gran's father was now back in the town they were from, on the Atlantic coast. He had been offered a month-long job there.

"What kind of work?" Gran asked.

"The same kind he had before. Fixing trucks," she said, but she seemed uncertain. Gran had the feeling that his mother did not have all the information she'd like to have.

"Something happened to the mailbox, too," his mother said. Gran had noticed it on the way in; it was crooked now, as if someone had pulled it to one side.

"So why are we here?" Maisie asked, then meowed. "We came here for work but now he's back *there* for work?"

"Nothing's for sure," Gran's mother said. "So we'll hold tight for the time being. Are you going to be a cat all night? I don't care, but I'd like it to be consistent."

"Meow," Maisie said.

After that, they ate in silence. In the past, when there was bad news in the house, bad news that Gran's mother denied was bad news, she was careful to make lively conversation. Often she'd play a game where she would ask Gran and Maisie which animal they'd rather keep as a pet.

"Okay, Komodo dragon or capybara?" she would ask.

"Capybara!" Maisie would say, though she could never remember what a capybara was.

"Okay, capybara or star-nosed mole?" their mother would say.

"Star-nose mole!" Maisie would say, though she had no idea what a star-nosed mole was, or quite how to say its name.

"Okay, star-nosed mole or mudskipper?"

The game could go on like that for an hour. Gran's mother had studied zoology in college, so she knew thousands of animals off the top of her head—and specialized in the strangest members of the animal kingdom.

But tonight she was quiet and ate little. Gran watched her mouth moving, though she said nothing. It was as if she was having some long silent dialogue with herself.

After dinner she said she was tired, and she wheeled herself into her bedroom and reclined on the bed, staring at a picture on the opposite wall. It was a watercolor of a rowboat on stilts by the shore.

Gran, unsure what else to do, sat at the edge of his mother's bed and thought about rubbing her feet. Hadn't she once said she liked that? But he didn't know how to do it, and she might not want that kind of thing at a time like this. So he sat with his hands in his lap.

Maisie crawled to their mother's bedside and meowed. Their mother reached down and petted Maisie on the head. Maisie purred, then said, "Fartmouth."

"Don't say that," their mother said.

"Meow," Maisie said.

"That's better."

It was still light outside, so Gran had an idea.

"Let's do Tidal Wave. I'll push."

"Meow!" Maisie said.

Back when they lived near the ocean, after school and before Gran's father would get home from work, they would walk to the beach and along the paved promenade, Gran and Maisie pushing their mother in her chair. They would go faster than usual, so they called it Tidal Wave.

The hills in Carousel were different. These were real. Their mother had to keep her hands on the brakes, and Gran didn't have to push much at all—it was more a matter of braking strategically. Gran jumped onto the back, and his mother gasped, and Maisie squealed, and the three of them barreled down the street like a runaway train. It was slightly dangerous and definitely unwise, but it put them all in a good mood, and Gran loved the feeling that he was driving, that he could control almost two hundred pounds of machine and human caterwauling down the road.

It was the happiest Gran had seen his mom in weeks.

Chapter TWENTY-FOUR

In the morning, the house was strangely silent. Usually Gran was the last one awake, but on this day, when he got up, he heard nothing. The sun was well above the purple hills on the other side of the valley, and his clock said 7:20, but no one stirred.

He went to his parents' room, where he found his mother in bed, Maisie curled into her arms and looking very much like the cat she pretended to be.

"I'm not feeling well," Gran's mother said. "Can you get Maisie ready for school? You know what to do."

Gran took Maisie into the kitchen, poured her cereal and added milk, and cut an apple and orange they could share. He made her lunch, then got her dressed and brushed her teeth. Gran was

67

putting on Maisie's shoes in the front room when he heard his mother's voice from the bedroom.

"Come say goodbye," she said.

They went into the bedroom to find her as they'd last seen her. She hadn't moved. She reached out and touched their cheeks with the backs of her long fingers. "Be sweet today," she said.

The second they stepped out of the house and closed the door, Maisie said, "I need stuff."

"What kind of stuff?" Gran asked.

"Poster board, markers, a ruler, and glue," she said. She'd been afraid to tell their mother, for fear of upsetting her.

"Okay," Gran said, reaching into his pockets for money. He found $6.21. "If we hurry, we can run to the store before school starts."

They ran down the hill and to the grocery store. They bought all Maisie needed, and Gran figured they could take a shortcut back up the hill and over to Carousel Elementary. From the window in their bedroom, he'd seen a stretch of woods extending directly from the shopping area to the school.

But when they got to the woods, there was a chain-link fence blocking the path.

"Look, it's that lady again," Maisie said. Hung from the fence was a YES ON PROPOSITIONS P&S sign, bearing the warm, smiling face of Phyllis Feeley.

"This way," Gran said, and they worked their way around the closed park, with Gran always keeping his eye on the rising sun

to the east. The park was dense with trees and foliage, and as they walked they could hear the scurrying of squirrels and birds in the thicket. Then the park grew less dense, and finally the greenery gave way to a wide expanse, with a lake in the middle of it.

"Is that a swimming pool?" Maisie asked.

Gran was trying to figure it out. It was an enormous rectangle, bigger than any swimming pool he'd ever seen, and it was half full of dull-colored water. Around the edges were tangles of steel cable, and strewn about were a few fallen doors and what looked like the remnants of a giant sign.

"It says CAT! See?" Maisie said, now holding the fence and bouncing on her tiptoes. As far as Gran could remember, this was the first time Maisie had recognized a word on her own. No wonder that word was CAT.

A gust of wind came down the hill and pushed the water across the pool and toward its northern side, and when the water moved, it revealed strange shapes in the pool. Gran squinted. Could that be the head of a horse?

"Ew!" Maisie squealed.

"It's not real," Gran said, though he couldn't be sure. What he was sure of was that there was a horse's face rising up from the surface of the water, as if struggling to breathe.

But it wasn't moving. It couldn't be real. Or alive. It was some kind of toy, like the rides in front of grocery stores.

"It's just an old toy," Gran said. "Let's go."

Chapter **TWENTY-FIVE**

66**S**ounds like you found the old factory, Grant," the Duke said at lunch. They were in his office, and the Duke had somehow found a sandwich bigger than the one Gran had seen him eat before. This one was as big as the Duke's leg. "You do know why this town is called Carousel, don't you?"

Gran hadn't ever thought of it. "I know the word *carousel,* but . . ."

The Duke's eyes were wide and white. "You don't know anything about this place, do you?"

Gran shrugged. The Duke paused, and Gran was sure the Duke was about to sigh in a way that would make Gran feel ignorant. But instead, the Duke smiled benevolently.

"That's why I laughed when you said the thing about merry-go-rounds. I thought you knew, buddy! This town used to be the foremost maker of carousels in the world. Carousels might have been invented in Europe, but they were improved in America. And they were *perfected* here."

"So the town made tons of carousels and sold 'em?"

"No. Not tons. Making a carousel takes time. At its height, the Catalan Carousel Company built about ten a year. And that took two hundred people, working full-time. But those carousels were beautiful. We sold them all over the world. We even shipped one to Turkey! Wait, look."

The Duke ambled over to a file cabinet, opened a drawer, and rifled through it. He pulled out a folder and opened it. He looked down and smiled. His eyes welled.

"This was the last one we built," he said, handing the folder to Gran.

The folder contained a dozen photos, most of them in black-and-white, of a carousel in various stages of construction. Men working on the complicated gears and engine that made the carousel turn. Women and men carving and painting the horses, zebras and giraffes that rose and fell as the carousel turned. Finally, there was a picture of a hundred or so people surrounding the finished carousel. It stood in front of a stately white structure with columns and a golden dome on top. It looked familiar to Gran. He'd seen this building, he was sure, though it looked different now.

"That's City Hall," the Duke said. "Not that you'd recognize it

anymore. But back then it was something. And in front of it, we built our most magnificent carousel."

"Where'd it go?"

"The City Hall one? No, we couldn't save that one. But before it . . ." The Duke trailed off. "While it was standing, though, people came from *Europe* to see it. I once met a man who didn't speak a word of English. But he'd come over on the *Queen Elizabeth*, then took a train from Boston all the way here. Got off, took a dozen pictures, and got back on the train. I think he was from Finland."

Gran looked closely at the picture with all the workers surrounding the newly christened carousel. Right in front, with his hand on the head of a bucking horse, was a very young and very short man who looked a lot like the Duke.

"That's me!" the Duke roared. "Good eye!"

"You worked there?" Gran asked.

"Of course I did. Everyone did. Everyone in town had something to do with the business. There were carpenters, engineers, glassmakers, painters, welders, truck drivers, foremen, shipping clerks, secretaries. And then there were the carvers. I was a carver."

"What does that mean?"

"What does *carver* mean?" The Duke's eyes were round and alarmed. "It means I *carved* things, Grant! I carved the animals. The molding. The poles."

"Out of wood?"

The Duke's eyes went from wide to wider. "Of course from wood! What else would it be?"

Gran thought of the animals he liked to mold from clay. Was that carving? He wasn't sure.

The Duke's eyes closed. "Well, later on, sure, they were made of plastic and aluminum. They started just using molds, and they all looked the same. But that wasn't what the Catalan Carousel Company did. Here, every carousel was one of a kind. Every horse, every animal, every pole, every saddle. Everything, one of a kind. You'll never see two of any Catalan animal anywhere in the world. Look at this," he said, and pointed to the horse he was standing next to in the photograph, the one rearing. "Know what that's called?"

"A horse?"

The Duke laughed. "Of course it's a horse. But this one is special. First of all, all the animals on the outside of a carousel platform were on what was called the Outside Row. They were always the fanciest, because they were the most visible. And the right side of any animal was called the Romance Side, and they were the most decorative for the same reason—they were the most visible. So you're seeing the Romance Side of the Outside Row. But then on top of all that, this was what was called the Lead Horse.

"This one's name was Gussie. The Lead Horse was the most elaborate, the most carefully made. Gussie here was also a Stargazer, which means she's got her nose pointing to the heavens. She was my favorite of all the horses I carved."

"So what happened?"

"To Gussie? She was on the City Hall carousel when . . ."

"When what?"

"Anyway. After a while, no one wanted carousels anymore."

"Why?"

"Roller coasters, for one thing. There was a time when carousels *were* the roller coasters. They were considered pretty wild. People used to get sick on 'em. A lot of people thought, *No, too crazy for me!*" The Duke laughed loudly about that. "Then roller coasters came along, and carousels were seen as too tame. So the orders dropped off, and pretty soon the factory had to let most of its workers go. It was a sad time, Grant. Then one night, as the town slept, we heard a loud commotion down by the factory, and in the morning we found everything had been swallowed up. The earth under the factory just collapsed, and the entire factory fell in. It was such a mess, and during a wet winter. Rain and snow fell overnight—too much to handle. Nothing was salvageable. That was that."

"So you started working at the school?" Gran asked.

"Eventually, yes," the Duke said. "I was too old to ride horses, and no one wanted me to carve them. I was lucky to get this job. But lots of people weren't so lucky. They'd come from all over the world to make carousels, and suddenly no one in the world wanted them."

Chapter **TWENTY-SIX**

O n Friday, Catalina was back in school, but Gran had no chance to talk to her. She'd arrived late to class again, spent fifteen minutes getting her yellow slip, and returned just before the period ended. When the bell rang, she was gone like a ghost.

That afternoon, Gran was committed to finding out where it was she went every day after school. He'd done his homework during lunch so he could leave his rollerbag in his locker. He wanted to be unencumbered and agile as he set off after her.

Outside, the wind swirled and changed direction and kicked up dirt. Branches fell from trees, birds scattered in all directions. The sky was an unhappy blue.

From the foyer, Gran watched Catalina burst out of the school and down the steps, across the street, and into the woods. She was moving quicker than she ever had before.

Without his rollerbag, though, Gran kept up without difficulty. In fact, because it was so dark that afternoon and there was so much chaos all around, he followed closer, knowing he would not be noticed amid the noise of the wind and leaves and falling branches. His eyes watered in the cold air. His nose wrinkled at the smell of wet earth.

As Catalina crossed the first valley, he found himself creeping up behind her, no more than fifty yards away. He was startled by a crash in the thicket nearby. A giant deer leapt out and across the path. Then another. And another. They were all enormous, gray, smelling of animal sweat. His mother had promised he'd see deer here, but he hadn't expected them to be so near, and so capable of crushing him underhoof. But they had no interest in crushing him underhoof. They were gone in a blink.

When they were gone, Gran gathered himself and located Catalina again. She was still striding quickly, now a few hundred yards ahead. He could see the sleeves of her flannel shirt billowing behind her. Occasionally, as she cut across a path, he could see her eyes, squinting and fierce as she strode.

A crack sounded behind him and he turned to find that a large branch had fallen a few feet away; had he been even a few steps slower, it would have flattened him. He turned back to the path and saw that Catalina had stopped and was looking directly at him. The sound of the falling branch had drawn her attention. Gran froze and his stomach dropped into his right shoe. But when he looked closer, he saw that she wasn't, in fact, looking at him. She was looking in his direction, but her stare was vague, focused on something beyond him or above him.

She turned quickly, and continued on.

Gran followed. He decided he didn't care if she knew he was following her. It had been a week since she'd spoken to him behind the school, and now he was beyond caring about being polite or timid.

He ran toward her.

Her back was turned and she was striding purposefully, about to round the bend where she had disappeared before. But this time Gran was running. His eyes watered, his legs ached, but his arms continued to pump, and he saw her grow closer in his sights. Now he saw her obsidian hair, how it shone just as brightly on this dark afternoon as it did on sunny days.

And then he saw something in her hand. It was metallic, shining brightly in the sun. It could be a knife, he thought. Or it could be a pen.

But then again, it didn't look like either of those things. It was silver, and curved, and what it looked most like was a handle. A handle without a door.

He ran closer. He found himself no more than twenty feet away from her, and twenty feet away from the hill behind which she had last disappeared. He saw then that it was indeed a handle: it could be nothing else. It was an ornate silver handle, bent like a sliver of moon. It was the kind of handle that might have opened a medieval castle door. He sped up, seeing that she was about to turn the corner.

But he wasn't fast enough. She disappeared behind the hill, and when he rounded the bend, he saw no sign of her. Again she had disappeared.

Chapter **TWENTY-SEVEN**

But this time, he saw something.

Right there, on the side of the hill, was an opening. A straight four-foot-high crack, about two inches wide. It was the kind of crack you see when a door is open, but only slightly. He crouched down to look inside, and when he put his eye to the crack, he saw what seemed to be a tunnel with Christmas lights strung along one side. The tunnel led to a wide cavern aglow with amber light. And descending down the tunnel and into the cavern was Catalina Catalan.

Then a sudden swirl of wind gusted from behind Gran, and the crack in the hillside closed with a thump.

He jumped back. His heart pinballed.

Something had just happened, something very odd. Humans are good at knowing when something very unusual has happened, and when these things happen, we need a moment to get our minds around these happenings. Gran had just seen a doorway to a hill, and then had seen this doorway close and disappear. There could be no mistake about it. He was standing before a high hill, in front of a vertical wall, and there had been a door there moments before.

Okay, Gran thought. *Okay*.

You may be reading this, thinking that what Gran should have done at that moment was to turn and run, because this all was too weird and too dangerous for a twelve-year-old boy.

But Gran did not have these thoughts. His thoughts, instead, concerned getting the door open again, and helping Catalina Catalan. Because it seemed to him that a classmate who was descending a path inside a hollow hill would probably need his help.

So Gran went about trying to get the door open again. It didn't seem difficult; he knew where the opening had been. But now, as he ran his fingers up and down the hillside, he saw nothing. No crack, no evidence of a door. It was as if there had never been any opening at all. The hill was seamless, just a regular mass of dirt and grass.

Gran ran his hands all over the side of the hill, getting dirt under his fingernails and mud all over his hands. He stirred up the pathways of ants and worms, but saw nothing like a door.

It was impossible. Seconds ago, Catalina had entered this hillside through some door that was no longer there. Gran stood, breathed deeply. He found his eyes welling. He wasn't sure if it was the cold wind or his own frustration. Where was Catalina? Was she trapped inside?

No. She hadn't looked trapped. The last he'd seen of her, she was descending a stairway with the same confidence and purpose she demonstrated wherever she went. She knew exactly what she was doing and where she was going.

Chapter **TWENTY-EIGHT**

At dinner that night, Gran was there but not there. The food tasted like paste and the words his mother and sister spoke were muted, seeming a thousand miles away. The phone rang, and Gran understood that his father was calling and wanted to talk to him and Maisie, but Gran was too distracted. His mother let Maisie meow into the phone for a few minutes, but when it was his turn, Gran didn't feel like talking to his father. He brushed his teeth afterward and went to bed. Or maybe he didn't brush his teeth. He couldn't remember.

Gran couldn't sleep. The events cycled through his mind. He'd followed Catalina across the valley, turned the corner, and she was gone. He found the opening in the hillside and saw her inside—

inside the hill!—descending some earthen stairway in an amber light. Then the door closed and it was as if it had never been there.

But what if the door hadn't been there? What if she hadn't been there? The most logical explanation was that he hadn't seen any of this. That he'd followed her, gotten hit on the head with a branch, and had a bunch of bizarre daydreams.

But that was even more ridiculous.

He hadn't been hit by any branch.

He'd seen what he'd seen.

He knew Catalina had been there, and that the door had been real. It was as real as his bed, his house, his sister sleeping next to him.

He knew he would not sleep that night. He knew he would not be able to concentrate. Not until he figured this out.

So he sat up.

He put his feet on the floor.

And he made the most interesting decision of his life.

Chapter **TWENTY-NINE**

He got dressed.

He decided he would go back to the spot, that night, and prove that either he was crazy or that he'd actually seen what he thought he'd seen.

But he'd never left the house after bedtime before. His mother would worry. Then again, she was a sound sleeper. She never stirred when he or Maisie made noise in the night. She wouldn't wake up tonight, either—not even if he left through the front door.

He looked at the time on his digital clock.

It read 11:11.

He crept downstairs.

Through the dark hallway.

Around the dark corner.

And into the dark kitchen.

He decided that the creaky front door might wake Maisie, and Maisie might wake their mother, so he went through the dog door in the kitchen—they didn't have a dog, but the previous tenants had. He poked his head through, then one shoulder, then the other. It was good to be small.

Chapter THIRTY

He was out in the night. It was cold, and still blustery, the wind wild. The gusts went south, then north, then seemed to spin in place, making tiny tornadoes before giving up and moving in some new direction. The wind could not make up its mind.

Gran made his way to the side of the garage, where he'd left his bike, but found its back tire flat. It was almost a mile to the hill where he'd last seen Catalina. Could he really walk all the way there and back? He had no choice. This was a night where sleep was impossible.

So he set out, staying off the main streets; he didn't want some concerned parent or police officer to see him and wonder what he was doing out so late. He cut through parks and two graveyards and across the parking lot next to the abandoned mill. He saw animals run into the woods, he heard the hoarse barking of dogs, the shrill yowls of cats fighting.

And finally he arrived at the valley. He took the same path he

had earlier that day, but now, in the moonlight, all was stark, stage-lit. The shadows were black, the path the palest blue. He knew he should be afraid but some more powerful feeling within him—maybe purpose, maybe curiosity—was dulling his fear.

Before he rounded the corner of the final hill, he paused. The last time he'd been there he'd seen something impossible: a door where a door didn't belong. His only friend—it was so odd to think of Catalina Catalan this way, given they'd only spoken once—had disappeared down golden steps inside a hill. Now what would happen? It seemed that anything was possible. Explosions, aliens, talking trees.

But no. That didn't make sense, he told himself. This was a specific kind of strange. Asecret door, a path known by Catalina. He resolved to check the hill one more time and then, if there was still no sign of the door he'd seen earlier, he would wait. He would wait and see if it changed, if anything changed. He would wait for Catalina.

Chapter **THIRTY-ONE**

There was no door. Gran checked and checked, running his fingers over the hill like a lunatic.

So he sat. He sat in front of the hill, watching it. He felt silly, sitting there in the night watching a hill, but he knew he needed to stay—if only to think this through.

So he sat and stayed as the night swirled around him. He was cold and blew hot air into his hands. The wind continued to whistle. The musty smells of animals distant and near filled the air. The swoosh of air passing through a willow down the slope. The squeal of a car's brakes somewhere on the other side of the valley. Then a siren.

He checked his watch and saw it was almost midnight. His father had given him this watch; it was one of the few things Gran could remember his father personally picking out. Usually shopping for birthdays and Christmas was done by Gran's mom, who loved toys and parties, and always knew what to get and how to wrap it. But every so often Gran's father would take an interest in a gift. Two years ago, when Gran had asked for a watch, his father had given him this one. It had a silver face and a blue cloth strap, and to Gran it was the perfect weight, the perfect size, and unerring in its accuracy. On the back, Gran's father had en-graved GRANITE, MY ROCK. LOVE, DAD.

An hour earlier, Gran had thought it impossible that he'd ever sleep again, but now he felt his eyes growing heavy. He closed his coat around his chest and brought his knees to his chin. He shivered and felt the wind shoot through his clothes and through his skin, chilling his bones. He knew he was miserable. He'd heard the word *miserable* before, but only now did he understand what it meant. To be outside, and cold, and have no way to get warm: this was misery. It was ridiculous. He didn't have to be here. He had a home. It was warm and he could go to it. He didn't have to be out here freezing.

By midnight, it seemed obvious. He had imagined it. Had he taken a nap after school, on the couch, and during that nap had he dreamed of this hill and its secret door?

Yes. It was the only answer.

Chapter **THIRTY-TWO**

But it was the wrong answer. Now your narrator is speaking, and I am here to tell you that Gran did indeed see what he thought he had seen. He saw it as clearly as you saw him seeing it.

But the human brain does a funny thing sometimes. When we see something that so conflicts with our everyday expectations of the world, sometimes our brains find a way to explain it away, or even to forget it. And this is what Gran did this night, as he shivered in front of the hill where Catalina Catalan had disappeared.

He forced himself to forget what had happened.

But this was wrong. Forgetting something like that is wrong. It's never good to forget unforgettable things.

But in this case it was okay, because at that moment, one minute after twelve, the door opened again.

Chapter THIRTY-THREE

That is, where there had been no door, now there was a door. The grass and dirt and weeds of the hill moved outward, and the same golden light Gran had seen earlier that day was now, in the dark of night, shining out from the doorway.

Gran didn't move. He didn't breathe or blink.

The door opened a foot wide, and Gran saw a familiar boot emerge and land on the path. He knew this shoe, wet with fresh mud, was Catalina's. Then a hand emerged, holding the hill-door open, and finally the full form of Catalina Catalan appeared in silhouette. She stood, and then turned to close the door behind her. She did it silently, and when the door was closed—just like before—there was no sign that a door had ever been there. Still, she carefully ran her hands along the edge, where the door had opened, as if to disguise the last signs of its recent existence.

Then she turned around, saw Gran, and screamed.

She backed away against the hillside. Even in the dark, Gran could see the whites of her eyes.

"It's me," Gran said. "Just me."

Now Catalina had her hand on her heart and seemed to realize that it was just Gran. Just a boy.

"Why are you here?" she managed to say.

During his long walk, and during his hours of waiting, Gran had been rehearsing what to say to her. He was ready to tell her the truth.

"I've been following you," he said. "And earlier today I saw you go in there." He pointed to the hill, which now had no door. It seemed ludicrous that he would be claiming she'd emerged from it. "And so I came back tonight and waited."

She stared hard at him for a long time.

"I'm sorry," he said.

Catalina started walking away, back into town. He ran after her.

"This is bad," she said, striding purposefully through the moon-lit dark. "So, so bad."

"Don't worry," he said. "I won't tell. But what is it? Where'd you go? What's the tunnel? Who put the lights up? Where does it lead? What about that room?"

"Please leave me alone," she said.

"I promise not to tell."

"Go away."

Gran stopped. He never liked to be where he was not wanted.

"This is so bad," she said again and again as she walked away. "This is so so so so so bad."

Chapter **THIRTY-FOUR**

But Gran thought it was good.

Even as Catalina walked quickly away from him, down the path and through a patch of woods that Gran didn't know, he was happy. So many good new things had happened, and these things made him feel alive and very tall and very strong.

He'd seen her. She'd seen him.

There was actually a door to the hill.

There was a tunnel inside the door, steps leading from the tunnel down to a grand cavern below.

He wasn't crazy.

He wasn't invisible.

And most importantly, Catalina Catalan had spoken to him again.

So he walked home alone, snuck back inside, and dropped into his bed. He fell asleep sometime near daybreak. When his mother called him for breakfast, his head felt as heavy and full of mush as a prize pumpkin. He couldn't lift it off the pillow.

Was it Saturday? He couldn't remember.

It was Saturday. He yelled downstairs, begging to sleep more, and his mother allowed it.

But he didn't sleep. He replayed everything from the night before in his mind. He was electrified. Nothing like this had ever happened to him. Had it ever happened to anyone? He thought there was a real possibility that Catalina was the first to discover a new world, inside our normal world, and that he was the second.

Chapter **THIRTY-FIVE**

When Gran finally got out of bed, just before noon, he came down the stairs to find his mother and Maisie at the kitchen table, licking envelopes and applying stamps to them.

"Just in time to help," his mother said. She was in a bright mood. Her hands were busy, her eyes alight.

The envelopes bore the words Yes on Propositions P&S. Into the envelopes, his mother and Maisie were stuffing folded letters explaining the propositions and why they mattered. "Save Our Parks and Schools!" the letter said in bold letters. Gran was relieved. Over the past few years, he'd learned that his mother was happier when she was involved in the community.

Civic engagement, she called it. In their old town, she'd helped stop a power plant, located a mile down the shore, from polluting the ocean. During that campaign, she'd been a force of nature, working sixty hours a week, getting Gran and Maisie involved. They dropped off flyers all over town, and though not everyone agreed with them, there was something fun about all those doors opening, seeing his mother talking to all those strangers, making so many of them friends.

"I kept seeing the signs around town," she said. "So I called up Phyllis Feeley and she signed me up. I'm already on the Steering Committee. And already have a phone tree. Anytime anything happens in town that has anything to do with Propositions P&S, we call each other."

Gran was relieved to see his mother involved again, and relieved, too, to finally know what Propositions P&S were. But this was followed by confusion.

"Who *doesn't* want to save the parks and schools?" he asked her.

"You'd be surprised," she said.

The phone rang. Gran's mother answered. She spoke for a moment, and the conversation ended gently. The phone rang again, but this time the brief conversation ended abruptly. Gran's mother's face looked alarmed by whatever words had come through the phone.

"See, that was an example," she said, after composing herself. "The first call was from one of the supporters of P&S. She was very sweet. The second call was someone against P&S and for M&H. He knew I was helping P&S, so he said some mean things to me and hung up. People have lost their manners over all this."

"What *are* Propositions M&H?" Maisie asked. She didn't quite get the word *Propositions* right, though. Coming from her five-year-old mouth, it sounded more like *Popozinis*.

"Well, sweetie," Gran's mother explained, "remember how I said people who support P&S want to spend money on parks and schools?"

Maisie smiled and nodded.

"Well, there's another side, led by Dr. Walter Woolford. He's on the city council, and he says there's no more funding available for parks and schools.

He says that the money should go to other things that he considers more pressing."

"Like what?" Gran asked.

"Moose attack prevention," Gran's mother said. "That's what Propositions M&H are. He believes that the town is surrounded by moose, and that they are responsible for much of what ails the town. That's Proposition M—the acknowledgment that moose are a big problem. Accordingly, he proposes that the town should buy a helicopter, and have it fly over the town at all times, so we can see the moose before they get into the town to attack it. That's *H*, for *helicopter*."

"Wait," Gran said. "*Do* moose attack people and towns?"

"No," Gran's mother said. "Not that I know of. But Dr. Woolford has the town in an uproar about it. Some people are very scared."

"But are there any moose around here at all?" Gran asked.

"There is no evidence of any moose anywhere around here in recorded history," she said. "But Woolford says he's a doctor, and that doctors well know that prevention is the best medicine. He says this goes especially for moose."

As Gran's mother had been explaining the threat of a moose attack, Maisie's face had darkened.

"But what if they *do* attack?" she finally asked.

"They can't," Gran's mother said. "There aren't any moose within a thousand miles of here."

Maisie's eyes were now wet, and her face was red. "I want the helicopter!" she wailed, and ran up to the room she shared with Gran.

"Can you go up and see about her?" Gran's mother asked.

Gran was on his way up the stairs when the phone rang again. He heard his mother gasp.

Chapter **THIRTY-SIX**

"You'll never believe this," his mother said. She hung up the phone. "That was the phone tree. A house up the block collapsed. Look."

She pointed out the front window. Gran saw dozens of neighbors walking briskly up the hill.

"Can I go?" Gran asked.

"Yes, but stay safe," his mother said.

Gran ran out the door and followed the crowd up the road and over, in the direction of the school. He saw a hundred people massed at the corner. It was a confusing scene, because Gran was sure he knew this block, and that on that very corner was the narrow burgundy wooden house where the pair of sisters lived. But now there was no house.

When Gran got closer and squeezed through the throng to see what everyone was seeing, he saw the narrow burgundy house, but a disassembled version of it, like a puzzle dumped on the floor. There was a window over here, and over there a door. There was a part of the roof, attached to a part of the chimney. And in the mess, there were the remains of the two lawn signs, YES ON PROPOSITIONS P&S and its opposite.

The destruction looked a bit like the work of a twister. But Gran knew this wasn't tornado country—or earthquake country.

"Poor Thérése and Theresa," a woman in front of Gran said, blowing her nose into a pink tissue.

"Don't worry," another woman said. "They weren't inside when it happened."

Gran stood with the crowd, looking at the house while listening to the story. From what he could gather, the two sisters, who had lived together for almost forty years in that very house, had been fighting. It had gotten so bad that they had refused to stay under the same roof on any given night.

So one night Thérése would stay in the motel down the road. The next night, Theresa would return and insist that Thérése get herself other accommodations, so Theresa would stay with an old friend. This had been going on for months. Anytime they were in the house together, they would start arguing, about their dogs, but especially about Propositions P&S, M&H.

"Lucky they weren't there last night," a woman in the crowd said. "Their dogs, too. No one got hurt."

"I saw both sisters at City Hall," said a man.

"On either side of the aisle," said another.

"Fighting like tigers," said yet another.

"Moose," a voice behind Gran said. Gran turned to find a face that looked familiar. He had an enormous mustache. "This is what I've been telling everyone," the man said, raising his voice to address everyone in the throng. "This is clearly the work of a malevolent moose. Or many of them. Many malevolent moose, running amok. Had we had helicopters patrolling like I've been recommending, this wouldn't have happened. They would have seen this marauding mass of moose miles away."

"Oh c'mon, Walter," a woman in the crowd said. Now it clicked in Gran's mind. The mustachioed man was Dr. Walter Woolford, the proponent of Propositions M&H.

The woman who had addressed him looked familiar, too.

"Don't 'Oh *c'mon*' me, Phyllis," Dr. Woolford retorted.

That must be Phyllis Feeley, Gran thought. He'd seen their faces together, on signs on this very property, for so long it was both surreal and strangely natural to see them together in the flesh.

They continued to argue, getting louder, and soon other adults in the crowd joined in. There was heated discussion of moose, and helicopters, and money, and schools, and parks, and the town of Carousel, and what it needed most. Gran heard enough arguing at home, and felt that there were few things uglier than hearing grown people arguing in public. He began to make his way out of the mob when something caught his ear on the edge of the crowd.

"Sinkhole," a voice said.

The voice was coming from a very old man holding the hand of a very small girl. He leaned her way, and explained what had happened to the sisters' house. He had a wheezy voice, like a dying vacuum cleaner, but there was something about his humble and resigned manner that made Gran feel like he was the one who knew the truth.

"The earth beneath a home," the old man continued, "or beneath anything at all, gets compromised, gets hollowed out, and before you know it, it can no longer support the weight of a house. The house falls in." The old man sighed, and Gran heard the last words he said as he walked away, holding the little girl's hand. "Been seeing too much of this over the years."

Gran turned to leave too, and when he did, he saw someone he didn't expect to see again, and certainly not so soon—certainly not in the light of day.

It was Catalina Catalan.

Chapter THIRTY-SEVEN

Gran had no intention of talking to her. Or moving anywhere near her. He felt ashamed that he had followed her the night before, and felt she had every right to be angry with him. He expected her to turn and flee, as she had last night.

But now she was walking over to him, and then she was pushing through the crowd to get to him, and finally she was taking his hand and pulling him down the street. She led him away from the town and into the hills, and all the while Gran thought about her hand holding his hand. He thought about how coarse her hand was, how thick the skin of her palm felt, how rough. The way Catalina was holding his hand was not a way that could be considered romantic or even friendly, but she was holding it anyway and that was something.

He had no idea where they were going, and Catalina hadn't said a word the whole time they'd been walking. It was only when they were deep into the woods at the bottom of the valley, away from all eyes and ears, that Catalina stopped, got very close to him, and spoke.

"So are you working for the Hollows?"

"The what?" Gran managed to say. He had no idea what the Hollows were. It was incredible he could talk at all, because being alone like this with Catalina, so near he could smell her perspiration, the earthy smell of her flannel, had him dizzy and disoriented.

"How can you say you're not working for them?" she asked.

"Who is 'them'?" he asked.

"The Hollows. You know exactly what I'm talking about."

Gran didn't mean to, but he laughed. He laughed in a sudden loud burst. It was just a reaction to the cloak-and-dagger nature of Catalina's questioning.

A look of pure fury came over Catalina's face. Then her arm reared back and her fist plunged into Gran's stomach.

Chapter **THIRTY-EIGHT**

The world looks very different when your cheek is pressed to the ground.

And your body feels different when you can't breathe. When you are on the ground and you can't breathe, your limbs feel leaden. Your lungs seem to be breathing not air but straw. Your eyes feel wet with acid.

Gran made these observations as he writhed on the ground, feeling the pine needles on his face, gasping for air. And then, for the second time since he'd known her, Catalina Catalan was on her knees next to him, helping him recover. And it was at that moment that he finally figured out who the old woman on Catalina's T-shirt was. It was Ruth Bader Ginsburg, the Supreme Court justice. The

way Catalina was positioned gave him a close look at her face, and
it was almost as if, as Catalina rested
her hand on Gran's back, Ruth Bader
Ginsburg was there too. It was a
strange feeling, but not unpleasant.
Catalina began to move her hand ever
so slightly in circles on his back, and
even while Gran struggled for breath,
he knew it had all been worth it.

Soon he could breathe again, and
he sat up, and she sat across from him.
They were both sitting in the middle
of the forest on a bright autumn day. It all seemed so normal and
wonderful to Gran until he remembered that Catalina Catalan had
just punched him, and was accusing him of working for something
called the Hollows.

"I don't work for the Hollows," he said. It seemed a very strange
sentence to say, given he had no idea what it meant.

Catalina squinted at him.

"Then what were you doing there last night?" she asked.

"I followed you," he said.

"You followed me where?"

"I saw you disappear. So I stayed outside the hill. I wanted to
know where you'd gone."

"Nowhere."

Gran knew this was not true. "You went into the hill," he said.

"No I didn't," she said.

Catalina was doing something people sometimes do when they don't want someone to know something. They deny something even though any reasonable person would recognize their denial as untrue. Gran had seen what he had seen and he was sure about it.

"I saw a handle in your hand," he said.

"No you didn't," Catalina said.

"I saw a stairway," he said.

"No you didn't," she said.

"And a huge room," he said.

"Nope," she said.

"It was lit up like a church at night."

"No it wasn't."

By this point Catalina had risen and was standing over Gran in a threatening position, as if she might punch him again.

"You didn't see any of that," she said. "I was out jogging and came around the hill and tripped over you. That's all that happened."

"But—" Gran began.

This time she kicked him.

Chapter **THIRTY-NINE**

The funny thing about having the wind knocked out of you once is that sometimes, the second time, you're ready for it. Which in this case Gran was. When Catalina reared up to kick him—in the stomach, with her foot—he steeled himself. He curled into a ball, ready for impact.

Gran knew that punching and kicking is not highly evolved behavior. It demonstrates that the kicker or puncher hasn't fully developed the ability to deal with their temper, and to express themselves like humans do, as opposed to the way of cavepeople or wolverines.

As if hearing his thoughts on human nature versus that of animals, Catalina did not kick Gran very hard. It was not a direct hit this time—more like a grazing. She grunted, then stood, her breath heavy with frustration.

"I have to go," she said.

"Let me go with you," Gran blurted out. He was surprised by his own boldness, and the strength of his voice.

"You can't come with me," she said.

But there was something in her voice that held open the possibility that she would listen to him.

"Let me help you," he said.

"Help me with what?" she asked.

"With whatever you're doing."

"I'm not doing anything."

"You were inside the hill."

"That's crazy. You're crazy," she said, but she said it unconvincingly. Gran felt like he was making progress.

"You were in the hill. I saw you," he said. "I can help."

She looked at him hard. "Are you good at anything?"

Her face implied that she was doubtful. Gran thought of telling her about making little animals out of colored clay—he thought he was good at that—but he was fairly sure this wasn't a skill useful to the current situation.

Then a look came over her, as if an idea had occurred to her. "Can you get that wheelchair?"

"What wheelchair? My mom's?"

"I've seen you pushing her around on it. Can you borrow it tonight? Can you get it to the junkyard by 11:20 tonight?"

Gran quickly did the calculations. His mother's wheelchair typically sat next to her bed while she slept. She went to bed at ten. After she was asleep, he could sneak into her room and quietly roll the chair out of the bedroom. Then somehow out the front door. Then down the street at night, all the way to the junkyard—a place he'd never been. He didn't know the town even *had* a junkyard. And he had to go there two hours after he usually went to bed himself. It was an impossible task.

"I can do it," he said.

Chapter **FORTY**

Gran lay in bed that night, unable to believe what he was about to do. He was about to steal his mother's wheelchair and take it to the other side of town. To a junkyard. Only now, as he lay, heavy head on pillow, did he realize that Catalina might be asking him to actually throw his mother's wheelchair into the junkyard.

Was that her plan?

No. Why would she want his mom's wheelchair in the junkyard? Did she plan to sell it?

No. He trusted Catalina. But why did he trust Catalina, a girl he had seen emerge from a hillside? A girl who had punched him and kicked him? It made no sense. But he did. He trusted her.

So at eleven, when he was sure his mother was asleep, he rose from his bed, tiptoed down the hall, and opened the door to her room. She was sleeping soundly, as she always did. He stood in her doorway for a full minute, to make sure she was truly asleep. She didn't stir.

He thought for a moment about the rightness of taking his mother's wheelchair. He knew she needed it, and removing it from the house was a grave offense. But he was only borrowing it, the same way his mother often borrowed money from Gran, and even Maisie.

Once every few weeks, she would ask for five or ten dollars, for groceries, for batteries, for anything. "You won't miss it during the borrowing," she'd say, and Gran and Maisie would feel a little thrill at being useful in this way—that their carefully saved money now was crucial to the functioning of the household. They would always give her the money, knowing she never failed to return it, usually within a day.

Now Gran would do the same. He would borrow something that would not be missed during the borrowing. His mother wouldn't use the chair while sleeping, would she? And whatever Catalina was doing seemed important. Gran's mother would likely agree with the use of her chair this night. Surely she would agree.

He crept toward the chair and put his hands on its handles. He turned it toward the door. A loud squeak pierced the quiet of the room. He looked down at his mother, expecting her eyes to be open. But they stayed closed. Her breathing remained steady.

He rolled the chair quickly, quietly out of the room and into the hallway. And that's when he saw Maisie.

"What are you doing?" she asked. She stood in the hallway in her stars-and-planets pajamas. Then, as if remembering she was a cat, she said, "Meow."

Her meow had been loud enough to wake their mother, so Gran shushed her and turned to close the door to their mother's room. This gave him enough time to think of an explanation that might work for a five-year-old.

"I'm cleaning it," he said.

"Why?" she asked him.

"She asked me to."

"Why?"

"It hasn't been cleaned in a while. Why are you awake?"

"I thought I heard something. Can I watch you clean it?"

"No," he said.

"Why?"

Gran knew that Maisie's *Whys* could last a while. And he knew that once she was awake, she could be very difficult to put back to sleep. So Gran found himself setting the wheelchair up in the hallway, and then found himself pretending to clean it. Actually, he wasn't pretending. He got some spray cleaner from under the kitchen sink, and a roll of paper towels, and for ten minutes cleaned the chair. His sister was at first fascinated with the process, and then became bored.

"I'm going back to sleep," she finally said.

And after she was back in bed and Gran had tucked her in, he closed the door to her bedroom. He wheeled the chair to the back door and carried it down the wooden steps as quietly as he could. He stepped into the night. A bright three-quarter moon was above, casting sharp shadows.

Gran looked at his watch. It was 11:11. The junkyard was at least three miles away, and he was supposed to be there in nine minutes.

The only way to make it there in time would be to take the hill. There was a very steep hill that ran directly from his house into town. But this hill was too steep to ride a bicycle down. Or a skateboard or scooter. Too steep for anything, really—especially a wheelchair. He'd end up in a dozen pieces, strewn all over the road. You'd have to be a loon to ride anything down a hill like this.

Chapter **FORTY-ONE**

But it was the only way to get there in time. If he was late to the junkyard, Catalina wouldn't wait. And he'd lose the only chance he'd ever have of knowing what she was doing in the hill.

So he steadied the chair at the top of the slope and he took a deep breath. He looked down the road, plotting his course. If he turned regularly, pivoting like a skier, he could still travel quickly but stay in control.

Okay, he thought. *Okay.*

He plotted a second course, too—the course he'd take if he lost control and had to crash. He spotted bushes and shrubs on either side of the road that looked marginally less painful than if he were to skid across the road on his face.

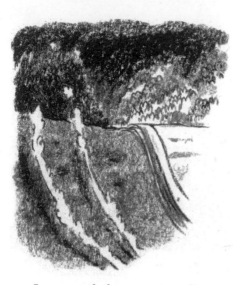

Okay, he thought. *Okay.*

Finally he was ready. He put one foot on the foothold, the one where Maisie usually rode. Then, with his right foot, he pushed off, gently.

The chair rolled slowly, squeaking slightly. Then it descended. The wheels took on new life, hungry for speed.

Wow, he thought. *Wow.*

In seconds he was traveling so quickly his eyes watered in the wind. He could barely see the road. He turned the chair, as he planned to—like a skier—but it was far harder to maneuver than he'd planned. The chair tilted, as if it would topple. He leaned away from it just enough, and just in time, to keep it on four wheels.

Oh no, he thought. *Oh. No.*

He must have been going thirty miles an hour.

He was going as fast as when his father drove them in the car. It was so fast he couldn't see anything clearly. There was a jumble of road, wind, trees, his hands. He thought of the times he'd wiped out on his bike, on his skateboard. First there was speed. Then a bump. Then the horizon line went diagonal. Then all command of limbs and gravity was suspended. The world spun and the ground flew up to smash his face and bones. This had happened before.

But this time.

This time the wheelchair tilted, and groaned and squealed, but Gran stayed calm. He leaned left and right, making minor adjustments to every bump and swerve, and somehow stayed upright. He flew down the main drag of town, through the outskirts and around that slow bend and that sharp turn. Gradually the road evened out, and Gran found—to his great surprise—that he was alive and unscathed.

In seven minutes he arrived at the junkyard.

He was two minutes early.

Chapter **FORTY-TWO**

"You made it."

Gran was in the middle of the road as the chair slowed to a stop in front of the junkyard's rusted gate. The voice came from the shadows. He knew it was Catalina. She emerged into the pale blue glow of the lamplight. She was wearing her usual T-shirt, her flannel around her waist.

"Are you okay?" she asked. "Your eyes look crazy."

"I'm fine. Just a fast ride here."

Gran looked at the enormous gate in front of them.

"Do you have a key?" he asked.

Catalina looked at him. "Sort of. Follow me."

She walked around to the dark side of the junkyard perimeter. Gran guessed that she planned to cut through the fence with clippers, and his stomach tightened thinking about being part of this. It couldn't be legal. His mom, if she ever found out, would be disappointed. She would be *devastated*.

But instead of turning toward the fence, Catalina turned away from it. On the other side of it, there was a hillside, and Catalina was examining it. Satisfied with her findings, she reached into her pocket and withdrew the same handle he'd seen before. It was silver, finely etched and sturdy.

She turned to Gran. "What I'm about to do is secret, okay?"

"Okay," he said.

"If you tell anyone about this, I'll never speak to you again."

"Okay."

"Worse, if you blab, you could be endangering a lot of people."

"Okay."

She took a deep breath. "I can't believe I'm showing you this. The Regional Manager would be so mad if he knew."

"Who's the Regional Manager?" Gran asked.

"Never mind. I shouldn't have mentioned him."

Then she lowered her hand toward the slope of the hill, stuck the handle into the earth itself, and when she pulled up, the hill became a door. Just as she had before, she'd created a door where there was nothing like a door. She'd revealed a hollow Earth through an impossible opening. Golden light shone from a rough-hewn tunnel.

"Hurry," she said.

Gran stepped inside.

Chapter **FORTY-THREE**

On the one hand, it was the most astounding place he'd ever been. On the other hand, it was just a tunnel, and looked a lot like the mining tunnels he'd seen pictures of in books. It was a tunnel right under the hillside, a tunnel seemingly dug by giant gophers, and was musty, dank, dark.

But it was lit by Christmas tree lights. The effect was crude and yet warm and welcoming, and everywhere along the corridor were vertical supports that seemed to be holding up the tunnel ceiling. But the supports weren't uniform, or even logical. They were an impossibly rickety network of broomsticks, hockey sticks and plastic pipes. It didn't seem feasible that these rods and poles were holding up the ceiling of the tunnel. But it couldn't be any other way.

"We have a lot of work to do," Catalina said. "So I'd rather not spend a lot of time explaining everything, okay?"

"Okay."

She turned her back to him, then turned around again.

"Where's the chair?" she asked.

Gran hadn't brought the chair into the tunnel. Catalina hadn't told him to. "I didn't bring it. It's out there," he said.

Catalina sighed loudly, pushed Gran aside, and with her handle held tightly, she reached up, attached it to the tunnel wall, and pushed outward. The darkness of the night outside was a door-shaped interruption of the warm glow of the tunnel.

"Can you get it?" she asked impatiently.

Gran retrieved the wheelchair and lowered it into the tunnel.

"Sorry," he said.

"Follow me," she said. "*With* the chair."

He followed her.

"I need the chair more than I need you," she said.

Gran wasn't sure how he felt about that statement, but he said, "Right. Of course." He followed her, pushing the chair along the rough floor, dodging the dozens of poles holding up the ceiling.

"We have to be quick," she said, and picked up her pace.

It was a crooked and meandering tunnel, and the random assemblage of objects made to act as supports—a child's plastic basketball hoop, a car bumper, two baseball bats standing, one atop the other—became stranger and stranger.

"Hurry, over here," Catalina said, and he rushed to catch up. She had stopped at a slightly wider part of the tunnel. "We're going outside again. Ready?"

Gran said he was ready, and like before, Catalina took her handle from her pocket, attached it to what seemed like a nondescript part of the tunnel wall, and pushed. The wall became a door, and the starry night was visible again.

"Let's go," she said.

Chapter FORTY-FOUR

They were inside the junkyard. Gran didn't know how he felt about sneaking in through the tunnel—it was better, it seemed, than cutting through the fence, but still it was trespassing.

"Okay," Catalina said. "Get anything you see that's about five feet tall that we can use as a support. Understand?"

"Like the columns inside the tunnel?"

She looked at Gran as if he were dense. "We need about fifty of them. When you get one, dump it into the tunnel. Then we'll use the wheelchair to get them to the area around the house."

"What house?"

"The one that collapsed. We have to prevent the damage from spreading. Are you paying attention?"

Gran was not sure what all this meant—collapsing, spreading, preventing—but he didn't want to tell Catalina this. He wanted her to think that he knew exactly what he was doing.

So with only the moon for illumination, Gran and Catalina rushed around the scrapyard, looking for anything tall and strong. Gran found part of a fence and threw it down through the doorway.

Catalina saw him, squinted, and Gran was sure she would disapprove. But she shrugged, as if to say *Good enough*, and he continued.

Catalina found another car bumper, and a tall post with a birdhouse still attached to the top. She found a hockey stick, and what looked like a javelin. Everything went through the open doorway and into the tunnel.

Gran worked without pause, finding twenty or so of his own makeshift columns, from an extra-long mop to what looked like a rusted metal chimney, and after an hour Catalina seemed satisfied.

"Okay. Let's go," she said, and jumped down into the tunnel. Gran followed, and she closed the door behind them.

Chapter **FORTY-FIVE**

Catalina showed Gran what she wanted done and how she wanted it done. What she wanted done was the stacking of as many of their columns as possible on the wheelchair. And she wanted it done carefully and quickly.

She was good at this, and Gran was not so good. As they worked, she made a series of dissatisfied sounds, like *tsk* and *hm* and *Oh lord no*. But soon enough they had arranged their findings on the wheelchair, and the wheelchair was ready to be pushed down the tunnel.

"Where are we going again?" Gran asked.

Catalina looked dissatisfied again, and refused to answer the question.

The silence was broken by the ringing of a phone. Gran knew it couldn't be his own, because he had no phone; his parents wouldn't let him have one. The ringing continued, a very loud and antiquated ringing sound that seemed to be coming from far down the corridor.

Catalina strode down the tunnel and reached for something high on a wall. It was an old-style wall phone, shiny and black. She picked it up. The receiver wrapped around her cheek like a parenthesis.

"Yes?" she said in a professional tone.

She nodded a few times and said, "When again?" and then, "That's in less than a week. How do you expect—" She nodded a few more times and hung up.

She turned back to Gran. "We need to close off and clean up the old-lady sinkhole."

"Who was that?" Gran asked. "The Regional Manager?"

"Yes. No," Catalina said. "There's no such thing as the Regional Manager. Or a phone in that tunnel. You didn't see anything. Okay?"

Gran had no choice but to say "Okay."

"Help me push," she said.

Gran helped her push the wheelchair, which was carrying about a hundred pounds of makeshift poles and columns, and objects that resembled poles and columns.

They pushed the chair through the tunnel as it turned left and turned right and inclined upward and downward and occasionally split. Catalina always knew where to go. Occasionally the ceiling was taller, occasionally it was shorter. But everywhere it seemed like a tunnel carved by a giant earthworm, or a wind blowing steadily for a thousand years.

And everywhere they went, they pushed together, side by side, Gran feeling very good to be so close to Catalina. He felt so good next to her that he forgot about all the questions piling up in his head. Why there was a phone in a tunnel. And who had made this tunnel. And why the tunnel existed in the first place. And why they were in it. And why they were pushing column-like objects on a wheelchair through the tunnel.

And exactly where they were going.

Chapter **FORTY-SIX**

"Where are we going?" he asked. They'd been walking through the tunnel for what seemed like a mile.

"It doesn't matter," Catalina said. "We're here." She stopped pushing so suddenly that Gran bumped into the chair and into the assemblage of poles sticking out behind it.

"Ow," he said.

Catalina looked at Gran as if his pain were absurd, as if he himself were absurd. "Anyway," she said. "As you've probably figured out, our job is to place these columns strategically so the tunnels don't collapse anywhere else. Watch."

Catalina took a two-by-four from the pile and pushed, pulled, and arranged it until it was standing straight up and down like a column, supporting the ceiling above.

"That really works?" Gran asked. The two-by-four didn't seem strong enough to support what must have been ten thousand pounds of pressure from above.

"Why would we be doing it if it didn't work?" Catalina asked, and took another long pipe from the pile and walked down the tunnel. "Are you gonna watch me the whole time or are you gonna help?"

Gran took a long piece of white plastic pipe and hoisted it onto his shoulder. He found an area of the tunnel where the roof sagged and tried to do what he'd watched Catalina do. When he had put the pipe into position, making it snug at the top and bottom, he stepped back to assess his work. It didn't seem possible that the pipe was holding up the ceiling. Then again, it looked sturdier than it had before he'd done it, and maybe that was enough.

In this way they worked through the night.

Finally, when it seemed like it must be morning, and when his shoulders ached and his legs were leaden, he asked Catalina if she knew what time it was.

"Probably five or six a.m.," she said.

Gran panicked. His mother usually woke at six. He knew he had to get the chair back into the house and by her bedside before she woke up.

"I have to go," he said.

"That's fine," she said.

"Where do your parents think you are?" he asked.

"Parent. My mom works the overnight shift at the grocery store. She gets home at seven. She'll never know I'm gone."

"And how do I get out?" he asked.

With a heavy sigh, Catalina led him through the tunnel, took a left, then a right, then they ran for a few hundred yards straight, then another left and right and stopped.

"We're in your backyard, next to your garage," she said. "Do you have a dog?"

"No."

"Good. Ready?"

Gran nodded, and Catalina took her handle from her pocket, attached it to the tunnel wall, then pushed. The light outside was dawn's pale gray, and Gran saw the sorry blue wall of his garage, and the familiar trees and shrubs of his backyard. He couldn't fathom how Catalina knew the route to his house. He didn't know how the tunnels worked, how the handles worked. But he knew, from Catalina's impatient look, that now was not the time to ask.

"See ya," she said, and pushed him through the doorway, sending the wheelchair after him.

Gran was in his backyard, behind his garage. The door in the earth was closed, and as always there was no sign whatsoever that a door had ever been there.

Chapter **FORTY-SEVEN**

He peeked around the garage and looked up to his mother's window. A yellow light. She was awake. By now she would have noticed that her chair was not by her bed. How would he explain that?

At the back deck, he grabbed the hose and quickly washed off the chair, and with a rag he dried it. When he was finished, it didn't look very good. In fact, it looked like it had been through some hard labor. Still, he had no choice but to rush it into his mother's room.

He made it as far as the kitchen, thinking desperately of a way to explain it all without lying—he was pretty sure he'd never lied to his mother and didn't want to begin this morning—but there was no way to explain the disappearance of the chair without revealing

too much. She would never believe what he'd been doing all night.

"Gran? Come in here please," she called.

Hearing his mother's stern voice, Gran felt a strange sense of relief, knowing that he'd been caught and would have no choice but to tell the truth.

"Coming!" he said, leaving the chair in the kitchen.

When he turned the corner, and could see her open door at the end of the hall, he also saw Maisie, standing next to his mother's bed, giving him an enigmatic look.

Gran entered his mother's room. She was sitting up in bed, wearing her usual sky-blue nightgown.

"Hi," he said, standing in the doorframe. "You up already?"

"I am," she said. "Maisie here says you took my chair?"

Gran felt his legs buckle. He knew his mother's next sentence would include *devastated*, and he didn't know whether he could bear it. But instead she said: "She says you were up late last night cleaning it?"

Again Maisie gave Gran that enigmatic smile, a smile that gave no clue whether or not she had believed her older brother. Maybe she *did* believe him.

"I did clean it," Gran said, realizing this wasn't quite a lie. He had just wiped it off seconds ago, on the deck.

"Can I see it?" his mother asked.

"'Course," Gran said. "But I'm not done. Can I bring it around in a few minutes?"

"I do need to start my morning," she said, "but I'll give you some time. I can't wait to see what you've done."

Gran, energized with the strange new idea that he wouldn't actually be in trouble—that with his sister's help he might actually be in the opposite of trouble—stopped in the kitchen, got a spray cleaner from under the sink, and a roll of paper towels, and went at the chair with a vengeance.

He cleaned the seat, the wheels, the spokes and footholds. When it was done, it looked at least as good as it had when he'd borrowed it.

His mother wasn't so sure. When he brought it to her, she tilted her head and squinted her eyes. "I appreciate your effort so much, Gran," she said. "It's so kind and thoughtful of you to think of surprising me like this, especially with things so hard around here lately . . ." She paused and her eyes welled. She sighed and gathered herself.

"But next time you should think of a less abrasive cleaner. Look at these marks," she said, and pointed to hundreds of scratches on the seat and armrests.

Seeing them, Gran knew they were caused by the poles and columns and two-by-fours he and Catalina had loaded. He swallowed a lump of guilt.

"Okay," he said. "I will."

His mother's shoulders shook, and he feared she was crying. Sometimes, over the years but especially in the last few days, he found her crying. Crying while opening the mail, crying while talking to her sister, Gran's aunt, on the phone. But she wasn't crying now. She was shaking, and the headboard behind her was shaking, too.

Chapter FORTY-EIGHT

"Get down!" she yelled. Gran and Maisie dropped to the floor, kneeling, and the ground under Gran's hands shook.

"Mama, is this an earthquake?" Maisie asked.

"It must be," she said. "But I don't see how that's possible."

Then it was over. It had lasted no more than a few seconds, but the effect was profound. It altered Gran's belief in the stability of things. During the shaking, the walls were no longer vertical—they moved and blurred. The floor vibrated and seemed to move side to side.

"This isn't earthquake country," his mother said, and Gran's thoughts were confirmed. He'd never heard of any seismic activity here, or anywhere near here.

His mother led them to the kitchen, which she deemed the safest part of the house, and she called her phone tree friends, and turned on the television, looking for any news of what had just happened. There was nothing on TV, which seemed odd to her and to Gran.

But after a few more phone calls, the answer seemed definitive. It hadn't been a quake. It had been another sinkhole, this one far bigger than the last.

"Where?" Gran asked.

"Your school," his mother said.

Chapter **FORTY-NINE**

He ran to it. His mother didn't try to stop him. It was as if the two of them knew the conversation that would have happened—*It'll be dangerous; I'll be careful; Stay where the firemen want you; Of course*—and simply decided that saying the words was unnecessary.

So he ran, across the valley and up the slope, wondering how much of the school was gone, whether his locker was gone, whether he'd lose anything important, whether anyone was in the building when it had happened, whether anyone had been hurt, whether Catalina would be at the school when he arrived, and whether or not she'd know anything about how this had happened. He knew she would.

The Duke! He thought about the Duke. What if he'd been inside the building when ... Gran ran.

As he scampered up the hill, he could hear the bips of police cars, the distant sirens of arriving trucks and ambulances, bursts of urgent words from loudspeakers.

When he arrived at level ground and could see the facade of the building, at first he was relieved. There seemed to be no damage. It looked exactly as it always looked—the narrow white columns, the red brick, the tall narrow windows covered with encouraging words

and celebrated assignments. He scanned left and right and saw nothing at all unusual.

"No one inside when it happened," he heard a fireman say. "That was pretty lucky."

Gran was relieved. He assumed the Duke was safe.

But where was Catalina? He figured she would appear.

But even if she was there, it would take time to find her. There were people everywhere. Police officers, firemen, paramedics. They were running left and right, holding axes, shovels, walkie-talkies. Gran stayed across the street amid a growing crowd of people. He recognized students he'd seen in school, their parents, some in pajamas and robes. All were craning their heads to see the damage, but there from the street, no damage could be seen. He heard the confusion from the throng:

"Maybe it wasn't so bad?" one woman wondered.

"Must have been in the basement," one man said.

"This is exactly why we need Propositions P&S," said another.

"Just the opposite!" yelled another man. "Only one force of nature could have done this, and that's a moose. Moose, plural. Maybe a dozen of them. They travel in small armies, as you know. This is exactly why we need Propositions M&H!"

The argument grew louder, and took in most of the people watching the rescue workers. Opinions seemed evenly divided, too, between those who wanted to improve the parks and schools and those who wanted to prevent attacks from moose by monitoring the city with a helicopter.

The crowd eventually thinned, but Gran stayed, watching the rescue workers come and go for hours. He stayed because he thought he might see Catalina. It seemed only logical that she would be there—she'd been there after the house of Therése and Theresa came down.

But this time she did not appear.

Chapter **FIFTY**

G ran went home. It was Sunday, and he assumed school would be canceled. But the next morning, his mother was in his doorway.

"Get up. You have school today."

He couldn't believe it. She couldn't believe it. But he was already late, so he dressed and ate and was back at the school twenty minutes after he'd woken up.

As he walked up to the building, again it looked as if nothing had happened to it. From the front, there wasn't a brick out of place. No cracks or crumbles. No broken windows.

So he walked up the steps, passing a number of teachers who had assembled there, talking rapidly and urgently. He opened the door.

And almost fell into an enormous pit. Before him, beneath him, was a great yawning chasm as big as a hockey rink. Far beyond he could see the back wall of the school, and to his right and left he could see hallways that were intact, classrooms intact, but the middle of the school had dropped through the Earth. The hole before him was about thirty feet deep, a messy oval littered with bricks and tile and pipes, schoolbooks, desks and pieces of chalkboard.

"Just go around," a voice behind him said. He turned to find the principal, Ms. Druck. She shooed him with her hands, as if he were a puppy lingering too long after doing its business. "The new room assignments are posted near the cafeteria."

All around the hole there was yellow police tape, but otherwise there was nothing preventing Gran or any other student from falling into the pit. He skirted the hole, and made his way to the cafeteria wall, where he saw a typewritten sign, newly laminated:

IF YOU NORMALLY HAVE CLASSES IN ANY OF THE CLASSROOMS NO LONGER IN EXISTENCE, YOU WILL NOW MEET IN THE ROOMS BELOW:

THEN: ROOM 103—NOW: LIBRARY
THEN: ROOM 105—NOW: GYM
THEN: ROOM 107—NOW: CAFETERIA
THEN: ROOM 109—NOW: ROOM 110

Gran jotted down the new room assignments and went to homeroom, which was, he realized, in a classroom that had been unharmed.

"There is a hole in the school," Ms. Rhapsod said, as businesslike as ever. "Now please turn to page 88 in your textbook."

The next two periods were similar in their strangeness, in their mundanity, though one of his classes, health, was held in the cafeteria, which smelled of burned tomato sauce.

It wasn't until lunch that he had a moment to really think about what all this meant. He stood above the sinkhole, looking into its chaos—a chaos that no one seemed inclined to clean up—when he saw Catalina standing on the other side of the hole. He rushed to her.

When she saw him coming, she looked down, then left and right, as if assessing which way she could go to most easily escape him.

"What's happening?" he asked. "I don't understand."

She leveled her eyes at him and sighed, as if deciding whether or not to lie to him.

"It's the Hollows," she said, and Gran was happy she'd decided to tell him the truth—though he didn't know what the Hollows were. He was about to ask, but she was staring into the chasm, and thinking aloud. ". . . But two of these in one week is really new. I don't get it either. I have to ask the Regional Manager. Sorry. I have to go."

Catalina was already walking away.

Gran followed her. "Wait. I can help. I helped before."

She didn't slow down. "I shouldn't have gotten you involved. Just forget it, please. There's already enough trouble."

She walked faster, now looking around, distracted, as if another collapse might happen at any moment.

"Are you following me again?" she asked.

"No," he said.

"It seems like you are. I'm walking and you're right behind me. That's *following*."

"But you know I can help. I did before."

At that, she stopped, turned and set her eyes on Gran. "Actually, you can do something for me. Go into the boys' bathroom and see if there are any cracks in the floor."

Gran, thrilled to be given a task, ran down the hall and opened the bathroom door, only to realize that this was Catalina's way of getting rid of him. When he returned to the hole in the floor, she was gone. He peered into the void, reasonably sure this was where she had gone.

Chapter **FIFTY-ONE**

But Gran couldn't follow. There were teachers all around, students everywhere. He couldn't get down there without being seen and provoking a frantic rescue.

Only Catalina could have gotten underground without being detected. And only Catalina would know why this second collapse had happened. Or if she didn't know, she was surely trying to find out.

"Grant?" a familiar voice said. "I wouldn't do that if I were you." Gran turned to find the Duke behind him. "You were going to investigate that hole, weren't you?"

"No," Gran said. It was the closest thing to a lie he'd ever told the Duke. And worse, Gran was almost certain the Duke knew he was lying.

Gran couldn't look at him. They stood side by side, peering into the hole, the twisted wires and concrete, and Gran felt the need to tell Duke the truth. But when Gran turned to him, the Duke's eyes were wet.

"What's the matter?" Gran asked.

"I just never thought it would happen here," the Duke said.

Chapter **FIFTY-TWO**

Gran went back to class, but couldn't concentrate. Something about seeing the Duke so upset got him not just upset but enraged. And inspired. And needing to do something about the situation. He wanted to fix it, wanted everything to be better so the Duke would never have to feel like that again.

He knew he could help if he could get underground and follow Catalina. But first he had to *get* underground and into those tunnels.

After school he looked for Catalina, to no avail. He pictured her running through the tunnels, fixing things, alone. He wanted to be there too.

He needed one of those handles. Could it be that easy—to get a handle and do as Catalina had done, to lift the earth and make a door where none had been before?

It seemed ridiculous to even try. But he had nothing else to do. So he walked to the flea market by the grocery store, where he knew shoppers could buy any kind of old thing, any piece of machinery or antique.

The sun was setting when he arrived. The market, drenched in orange light, was a meandering mosaic of ramshackle booths and tents, each helmed by a lonely man or woman, invariably sitting in a folding beach chair. Gran passed a booth selling lamps, and one selling helmets, and one selling old guns, and finally found a sprawling booth tended by an old man with shoulder-length white hair. In the

sunset's low light, now pink, he looked like some ancient mutant—half-human, half-lion.

"Can I help you?" the man said. His voice was deep and his accent unfamiliar.

Gran scanned the offerings on the tables. There were piles of hinges, and keyholes, and doorknobs, all old and worn-out. Some of the bins had price tags on the outside, signs like ANYTHING HERE: $1 EACH.

"No, just looking," Gran said.

Gran continued to look through the piles. He knew he needed a tool that could pull something, but otherwise he wasn't sure what

he wanted. He was reasonably sure he would know it if he saw it. It should be ornate, he thought. And strong, with intricate designs on it. Something impressive.

"We don't get too many kids around here looking for this kind of thing," the old man said. "You looking for a particular piece of hardware? For Dad?"

"Just a handle," Gran said.

"You know what size or shape you're looking for?"

Gran shrugged.

"What are you pulling? A drawer? A cabinet?"

Gran shrugged again.

"A door?" the man asked.

"I don't know," Gran said. Gran had been moving down the table, and he'd noticed that the man had been mirroring his movements from the other side of the table.

"You have a budget?" the man asked.

"I have eighteen dollars," Gran said.

The man smiled with his mouth and his eyes, a satisfied and delighted smile, as if he'd cracked a secret that Gran had been trying to conceal.

With that, the man ducked into his trailer and returned with a wooden box bearing a strange insignia on its cover—something like a dragon with the face of a lion. He set the box on the table and opened the lid. Inside were an array of handles, all of them far more elaborate than the ones Gran had been sorting through in the bin. They looked much more like the one he'd seen Catalina use.

"This the kind of thing you're looking for?" the man asked, a mischievous light in his eyes.

"It is," Gran managed to say.

In the box there were silver handles, bronze handles and copper. They bore carvings and even jewels. One was covered in rubies and emeralds. Gran picked up each one, feeling its surface and heft. He lifted and replaced ten or twelve before he found a bright handle of polished gold.

"Not real gold," the old man said.

But otherwise it was magnificent. It shone gloriously in the last rays of the sun, it was as heavy as lead, and bore ornate markings that Gran assumed were connected to some centuries-old mystery.

"Is that the one?" the man asked.

"It is," Gran said. He was absolutely sure.

"Forty dollars," the man said, and Gran let out an involuntary sound, something like a squeak. He didn't have anything like forty dollars. He had eighteen in his pocket, and that represented all the savings he'd accumulated cutting lawns and gardening in his old town.

"I have eighteen," Gran said.

The man cocked his head and smiled. "That'll do it."

Chapter **FIFTY-THREE**

Gran ran from the flea market, down the street and into the hills. He had an inkling that Catalina could go underground anywhere she chose, but he figured for this, his first attempt, his best bet was the wide flat hillside where he'd first seen it happen.

As he ran, the weather darkened and the wind picked up. What had been a sunny day turned surly and cold. Just the kind of weather that had held sway when he'd first followed Catalina and realized her power. So he took this change in the atmosphere as a sign that this was meant to be, that the night was right.

He arrived at the spot out of breath. He looked all around and saw no souls, mammal or avian. He was alone. He took the handle out of his pocket and even in the darkening sky it still appeared regal, golden and aglow, a thing of power.

Then again, he felt silly. The act of attaching a piece of metal to a hillside—it seemed ridiculous. But he'd seen Catalina do it a dozen times, and when she'd done it, it seemed effortless and right. And he'd seen her pull a door out of the earth itself. It had to be possible. But could it be possible for him?

He crouched down, holding the handle tight in his right hand. He aimed it into the hillside and pushed it deep into the earth. He took a breath and pulled.

Nothing happened.

He pulled nothing back. Just his hand, holding the handle with some dirt and grass attached. Now he really did feel ridiculous. Out of habit, he looked around, expecting someone to have materialized just to see him do this dumb thing and laugh heartily.

But there was no one.

So he tried again. This time he pushed harder. He pushed deep into the grass, and felt something like rock beneath. Maybe this was the sign he'd made a connection. So he pulled back, this time ready to lift the full weight of a fifty-pound door.

Nothing happened.

Or rather, something happened, but it wasn't the right thing. He pulled so hard that he landed on his rear, five feet from the hillside.

Again he looked around, sure that someone had seen him, and again relieved that no one had.

He tried again. And again. He tried in that spot, and all over the hillside. It seemed nonsensical to keep trying, but just as crazy not to.

Chapter **FIFTY-FOUR**

Eventually he gave up. It was getting dark, and he was tired, and he was embarrassed. To be alone, in the middle of a barren valley, and still be embarrassed—that is an unusual level of embarrassment.

Gran was also unusually late. He checked his watch and saw that it was seven, which meant he'd missed the dinner hour, and would be in trouble with his mother.

He slumped home, jogging a bit, walking a bit, feeling dejected and confused. Catalina was gone, somewhere under the earth, and he couldn't find her. He couldn't do what she could do. And he'd spent his last dollar on a useless handle.

If tomorrow Gran's mother asked him to borrow three dollars for milk, what would he say?

I lost it.

It was stolen.

I spent it on a door handle.

He realized then that the man who had sold him this worthless piece of metal had known it was worthless. Once he'd known Gran had eighteen dollars to spend, he'd found some piece of junk that looked more expensive, and he'd tricked him into thinking it rare and wonderful.

And worth all the money Gran had.

It was worth nothing.

Maybe Gran was worth nothing, he thought.

A dope gets duped, his father had once said to him.

Gran felt like a dope.

He entered the house to find his mother and sister on the couch, watching a TV show about ballroom dancing. His mother didn't look up. Sometimes she confronted Gran when he'd misbehaved or come home late, and other times she said nothing and did nothing, as if she'd decided his misbehavior couldn't justify the ruination of her evening. Knowing she hadn't made him dinner—or if she had, she'd eaten it herself—he got a bagel from the fridge, covered it in peanut butter, and went to his room.

Chapter **FIFTY-FIVE**

Then he remembered something.

With the bagel in his mouth, he pulled the ladder from the ceiling, careful to do it quietly, hoping his mother would not hear.

He set the ladder on the floor and climbed up. He pulled the chain dangling from the single bulb that hung from the beam above. The attic filled with light and shadow. He found the box of his great-great-grandfather's tools and metalwork. He rifled through the box until he found something that he thought might work. It was the brass C he'd picked up when his father had first shown him the attic. The weight of it in his hand felt just right. It felt like it had been carved to fit his hand.

"Gran?"

It was his mother.

"Just a second!" he yelled down.

He rushed to the ladder again, and stepped quietly down. He brought the chair over so he could reach the attic door to close it. But when he stepped onto it, and was holding the door, closing it, the earth shook. It felt like the house had been picked up and rattled like a box of cereal. Gran held on tight to the attic door as long as he could.

But then he fell.

Chapter **FIFTY-SIX**

He hit the wood floor hard. A searing pain shot through his shoulder. Something felt wrong with his head.

"Gran? That you?" his mother called.

He raised himself to his knees.

"I'm fine!" he called out. "Just fell. Don't worry."

Instinctively he reached for his head and felt something hard. It was the brass C he'd found. It was in his hand.

The dull brass was now streaked with red. He used his other hand to touch his forehead, and found it was wet with blood. He sat up, and when he did, the pain in his shoulder screamed. He'd heard of people dislocating their collarbones, and Gran wondered if that's what he'd just done.

The other thing—and this was a different thing, a good thing that made the pain from his head and shoulder bearable—was that he felt suddenly but absolutely embraced by destiny. The handle in his right hand fit so tightly and so well that he was sure it meant something.

In the lives of humans, there are moments that feel very much apart from the majority of moments. That is, in any life there are many hundreds of thousands of hours and millions of minutes, and though those hours and minutes might be filled with contentment, or joy, or pain, few of them are bathed in the light of destiny. Very few of them feel as if one has been taken from their regular life and lifted into a new, extraordinary existence. It is these moments that bring an ordinary life into the realm of the extraordinary. It is these moments that are doorways from a life lived to eat and drink and sleep, into a life lived to do monumental things.

"Gran? You sure you're okay?" his mother called out.

He heard her start toward him—the wheels on her chair squeaked and gave away her movements—and he knew he couldn't have her see him like this. She would call an ambulance, she would worry, her night and the next few days would be occupied with caring for him.

He didn't want that. What he wanted was to test this new handle, so he stepped lightly down the hall and through the kitchen. At the kitchen door he yelled, "Going to the garage for a second!" and leapt into the night.

Chapter FIFTY-SEVEN

The night was warm and calm. He felt at home outside, even though everything in or near his left shoulder roared with pain. And even though there was a wound of unknown severity on his forehead. Even though he was barefoot.

He'd just realized he'd forgotten his shoes. He'd left in such a hurry that he hadn't put them on. He thought briefly about going back to get them—he knew they were right on the other side of the kitchen door—but he also knew that to go back inside was to invite his mother's worry.

So he stayed outside, in his bare feet, and with the brass C firmly in his palm.

Just then, Gran felt the sudden presence of Catalina. He knew he was alone, but at the same time he had the unmistakable sense that she was near.

He knew he wanted to join her and help her, and knew that to do so he needed to find his way underground. He didn't want to go all the way back to the hillside. So he stepped through the wet grass in his bare feet and ducked behind his garage. There he found the spot where he and Catalina had re-entered the world the other night.

He took a breath.

He dropped to his knees.

The ground beneath him was just dirt, a few stray patches of grass. But it had been a door just a few nights ago. Why couldn't it be a door again?

He took the brass C and pushed it into the earth.

Immediately he felt something like a click. There was no sound, but the handle seemed to grab hold of the earth. Gran positioned his legs and pulled, and the ground beneath him became a door. It was heavier than a regular door, but not by much. Opening it made no sound.

He'd done it! He'd opened a door where there had been no door. Holding it open, instinctively he looked around him, to make sure no one was watching. He peeked around the corner of the garage, and saw the window of the living room, his mother and sister's faces blue from the light of the television. They suspected nothing.

He turned back to the door, and saw the warm yellow illumination of the tunnel.

It occurred to him that he had no idea what he planned to do. He knew he wanted to look for Catalina, but he had no map, no sense at all of where he might be in the labyrinth underground, and where she was in relation to where he now stood. And if he went inside, was he absolutely sure he could get out?

No. He wasn't sure, not at all.

But he took a deep breath, and though it seemed utterly insane to actually enter the tunnels and close the door behind him, this is what he did.

Chapter **FIFTY-EIGHT**

As soon as he closed the door, the air seemed to tighten all around him. He felt his throat close up. He couldn't breathe. He felt claustrophobic, though he'd never felt this way before with Catalina.

Just minutes ago he'd felt so sure about going underground. He'd been bathed in the certainty of destiny. But now he just felt scared. He was alone and he had no idea at all what he was doing.

The tunnel was dimly lit, with Christmas lights hanging loosely from eye-hooks. The passage extended without end in either direction. But one way seemed brighter, and in this direction the tunnel seemed to open up wider as it unfurled into the distance.

This is the way he went.

Gran told himself that he would walk for a minute or two, just to see if anything became clearer—where he might go, how he might find Catalina. Catalina no longer felt close to him, but he also had the strong sense that what he'd felt moments before had been real: Catalina was not far.

He walked down the tunnel. Every few steps he saw evidence of her handiwork: A diving board standing vertically, holding the ceiling up. Then a piece of steel siding. Then a car bumper. A fake marble column, a pole-vaulter's pole. The tunnel widened, narrowed, bent slightly left and then right. Within minutes he had no real idea how far he'd walked or where he was in relation to his house.

And then he almost fell to the center of the Earth.

Chapter **FIFTY-NINE**

Gran was walking along a lesser-lit passage of the labyrinth when he sensed a cooling of the air. Something was wrong. Or different. Or both. Different and wrong and dangerous. Now the lights began to flicker.

He looked down and saw that his right foot was inches away from a hole. The hole was barely visible, an utterly black oval the size of his kitchen table at home. It seemed to be exhaling—a cool breath coming rhythmically. Gran crouched down and felt a gentle but cold wind, a wind that could have been traveling for miles before it arrived at this place in the tunnel.

Gran took a rock from the tunnel floor and dropped it into the hole to gauge its depth. He heard the rock flick a wall or two, but there was no end to its drop. The hole was a tunnel like the tunnel he was standing in, but this one went straight down, apparently without end.

Catalina had said nothing about vertical tunnels.

Then again, Catalina had said nothing about any of this.

He didn't know where she was or how he would find her. He didn't know how she would react when she saw him. And he didn't know what that sound was—the sound suddenly coming from the hole below.

Chapter **SIXTY**

The sound was a howling.

It was a rumbling.

It was like an earthquake hurtled forth by a hurricane.

And it was getting closer. It was coming up from wherever that hole led, and it was coming toward Gran.

He ran as if he'd been caught by surprise atop a volcano that was now erupting. Because something very much like that seemed to be happening.

He ran the way he'd come. He ran faster than he'd ever run, even though he was barefoot, and his collarbone ached, and his left shoulder could barely move. He did not turn around. He did not breathe.

But he could hear the sound getting louder. It was the sound of

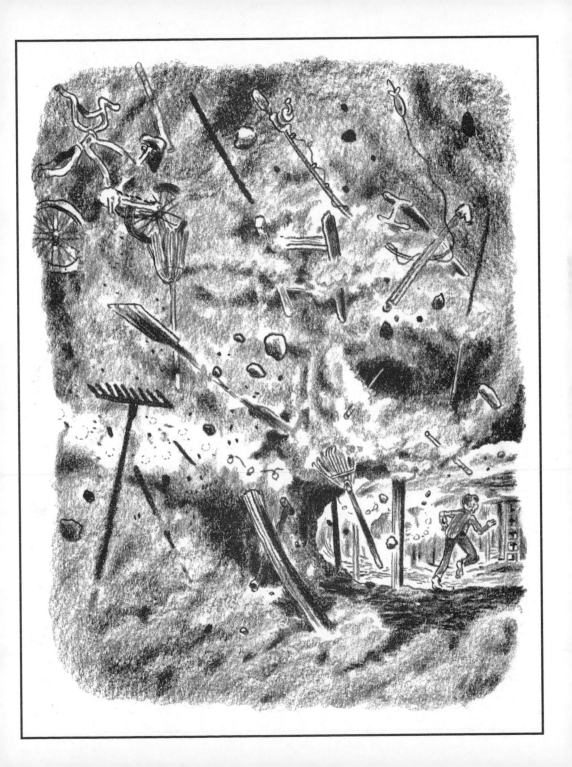

a wall of wind, carrying dirt and scree that scraped the walls of the tunnel with a rattling hiss. The wind roared maniacally, and when it seemed that it couldn't possibly get any louder, it grew five times louder, then ten. Gran continued to run, sure that the wind would overtake him any second, because the world around him seemed very much on the verge of ending. Then it got louder.

And finally he felt something. A pebble on his calf. Then the scrape of a rock shooting across his forearm. Then the thump of a stone landing squarely on the center of his back. All at once the dirt and rocks were everywhere around him, and he was aloft. The feeling was like swimming in the ocean and being taken under by a great crashing wave, when the water spins around and churns everything with its fury—the sand, the fish, the humans. Gran was in the air, being carried forth by a furious wind traveling at seventy, eighty miles an hour. He was spun around. He caterwauled and struggled to stabilize himself, to see anything, to feel the ground beneath him. But he had no control. He was just an object tossed about by this tunnel-borne hurricane, and he could only hope that—

Hope that what? That it would die out? Hope that he could exit somewhere, as a car would exit a highway?

And just as his mind fought with hopelessness—the part of him that said he had no chance to stop this, to free himself—just as he felt he had no choice but to float helplessly along until the wind died or was interrupted by some competing force, he hit a wall.

Chapter **SIXTY-ONE**

It had to be a wall. It hurt like a wall. Just as he'd done when he first tried to walk through the wall of his school, he felt the cruel result of human versus wall.

The wall always wins.

The pain was extreme.

The wind swirled all around him, louder than ever.

He felt like a lump of dough thrown against a marble counter. Every part of his body—even his ears, even his fingernails—ached. He realized, though, with some satisfaction that he was on the ground. Flattened, facedown, no longer moving. The wind had thrown him against a wall. Meaning the tunnel had ended. Meaning the wind, too, had hit a wall.

He savored the ground beneath him while the wind continued to swirl like a tornado in a cage. It seemed like a thinking being, an animal cornered. Then it began to retreat.

Gran couldn't believe it. He'd been in the throes of the wind in its mad journey through the tunnel labyrinth for so long—how long? It seemed like hours, though it was probably no more than ten minutes—so long that now, lying on the ground with the wind retreating, the noise diminishing, he had to adjust to not being tossed forward by the underground hurricane. He'd forgotten what it was to live without that kind of noise, that kind of encompassing chaos.

The wind continued to retreat in what he could only perceive to be a sort of frustrated mass of air and dirt. He knew that a force like this couldn't think, couldn't have a personality, and yet he had the distinct sense that this was some kind of being with a mind, with feelings, with intentions.

And because humans, as frail and simple as we are, have the strange and usually correct ability to sense things like this, Gran knew that he should listen to the voice inside telling him that this wind was a sentient force, and it was annoyed by the obstacle in front of them, this wall of dirt and rock.

The voice told him that the wind intended to go through this wall.

That it was retreating only to gather strength.

That it was getting a running start, and would soon attack the obstacle in front of it with a force tenfold stronger than the power it had shown thus far.

Gran knew how strange his conclusion was.

But he knew, too, that this conclusion was probably correct. And that he needed to move, somewhere, anywhere—he needed to get out of the path of the force reassembling itself.

But what could he do?

He thought of digging. No, not fast enough. He thought of running through the wind—maybe he could push through it and come out the other side? No.

Then he thought of the handle in his palm.

Of course. Immediately he jammed it into the tunnel wall and pulled.

It didn't work.

He turned and thrust it into the opposite wall. Nothing.

He tried the floor. Nothing.

He stuck it into a dozen places all around him and nothing happened.

And now the same sixth sense that had told him that this swirling mass of wind and detritus was a thinking force with its own distinct intentions—this same sense was telling him that whatever gathering of power it needed to do was now done and it was ready to come back at him, to throw itself against the end of the tunnel. That it intended to extend the tunnel by throwing itself against the wall, pushing through it, churning and obliterating it and everything in its path.

Chapter **SIXTY-TWO**

The howling grew louder. The hurricane in the tunnel grew angrier. The dirt spun around and pebbles shot toward him, fast as rabbits, hard as glass.

And then it sprang like a great cat, coming at him with a sudden ferocity. Gran crouched down, making himself into a ball, hiding his head between his legs. He closed his eyes and hoped for the best.

He assumed he would first be picked up, then thrown against the wall.

He assumed that the wind would churn and churn and cut its way through the rock wall and make a new path.

And he assumed that when it did, he would be carried forth as he had been carried before.

He did not assume that a door would open beneath him and he would fall through it.

And he did not assume that he would land on the floor of another tunnel, this one just below, and that when he gathered himself and opened his eyes, he would see the scuffed leather boots of Catalina Catalan.

Chapter SIXTY-THREE

"**I**'m confused by you," she said.

Gran looked up. Catalina stood over him, seeming calm but annoyed.

"On the one hand," she said, "you're the dumbest kid I've ever known. You almost got yourself killed by the Hollows. I've been doing this for two years and I've never gotten as close as you just did. So you're stupid. On the other hand, you're lucky, which, come to think of it, a lot of stupid people are. That's the only way they can survive."

Gran tried to speak, but the breath had been knocked out of him. He'd fallen six feet and landed on his ribs. He'd never broken a rib, but he was fairly sure that he'd at least bruised one now. Or it could be just his collarbone, probably dislocated, asking for his attention.

"On the other other hand," she continued, "you somehow figured out how to get into the tunnels. And you somehow survived a direct encounter with the Hollows, which I didn't know was possible. So that means you're either not just regular lucky, but incredibly lucky, or it means you actually have a brain."

Gran's lungs were regaining the capacity to breathe, but Catalina was still debating Gran's intelligence. She was thinking out loud, as if Gran were not lying in front of her, gasping for air.

"Then again," she continued, "the first time I met you, you had just walked into a wall. So you can see how confusing you are. And by the way, why are you barefoot?"

Finally Gran had the opportunity and ability to speak. He didn't bother to try and answer any of Catalina's questions, because he had a question of his own, which seemed more urgent than hers:

"What just happened?"

Chapter SIXTY-FOUR

"You *know* what happened," Catalina said.

"I don't," Gran said, but now he was unsure. Maybe he did know?

"You know exactly what happened," she said. "In your gut, you know." Now she turned her eyes to the ceiling of the tunnel. "Why do people always need things explained when they're so obvious?" She turned back to Gran.

"I told you about the Hollows, didn't I?"

"Yes," Gran said.

"And what are the Hollows?"

"The wind that attacked me?"

"What you just said was a question," she said. "I need an answer. You know the answer."

"The Hollows—that's the wind that attacked me," Gran said.

"Right. But did it attack you, or were you just in the way?"

"I guess I was just in the way."

"What do the Hollows do?"

"They tunnel through the Earth."

"Good. And what happens to factories and houses and schools sitting above these tunnels?"

"They collapse. They fall in."

"Good. And who tries to prevent all these things from collapsing and falling in?"

"You?"

"You doubt this?"

"No."

"So why did you say it like a question?"

"Sorry. You. *You*. You try to stop the collapsing."

"Of what?" Catalina asked.

"Of everything above."

"Say it as one sentence."

"You try to stop the collapsing of everything above."

Catalina almost smiled. "Right. And why me?"

"I don't know."

"Think about it."

"Because you're small enough to fit in the tunnels? Because someone has to do it?"

Catalina tilted her head and this time she actually smiled. A crooked smile overtook her face.

"Good," she said. "That's good. That's a start at least, and I'm impressed. Now the big question: Why do the Hollows do all this?"

Gran searched his mind and found nothing like an answer. "I don't know," he said.

Catalina's smile disappeared. "Shoot," she said. "I don't know either. Part of me thought you might actually know."

Gran and Catalina stood there, looking at each other for a long moment. The silence was profound, and Gran felt many things at once. He was baffled by Catalina, her power and her responsibility. And he felt strangely confident: he had shown Catalina that he knew a few things, and could survive amid a small

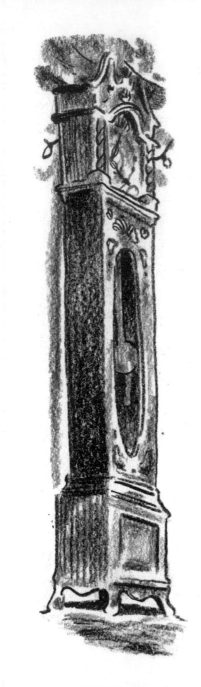

hurricane screaming through a narrow tunnel deep under the earth.

He also felt great pain, a dull pain throbbing all over, and remembered how he had done something nasty to his collarbone, had run into a solid wall with his head, and had, most recently, broken or bruised a rib. But stronger than any of these feelings was the feeling that he had gained some measure of respect from Catalina, the closest thing he had in the world to a friend.

He was in the middle of this brief and happy reverie when a ring rattled open the quiet. It was another one of the old-fashioned telephones.

Catalina calmly turned around and walked to a wall phone that Gran hadn't seen until that moment. She picked up the receiver but didn't say hello.

"Yup," she said, and looked over at Gran. "I know. I know. I know. Yes. No. No. No. No. Of course not. Okay. I'll get rid of him. Yup. No problem."

She hung up and looked at Gran.

Chapter **SIXTY-FIVE**

"**D**on't worry," she said. "I don't agree that we need to get rid of you."

"Get rid of me how?" Gran asked. "Who was that on the phone?"

Gran had no clue what he should be doing. Should he run? Could he run? He had nowhere to run.

"It's not like I'd kill you or anything," she said. "That's not what he meant. He just meant that I need to get you out of the tunnels and maybe erase your memory or something like that."

"Erase my memory? How?" he asked. Did Catalina really have the power to erase memories?

"He didn't actually say anything about erasing your memory, but I'd love to have that power. Wouldn't you? But I'm just a Lifter. You dropped this, by the way," Catalina said, and in her outstretched hand Gran saw the brass C. "Where'd you get that? Looks like a horseshoe."

Gran didn't know what to say. Catalina was talking so casually about having people's memories erased. Who was on the other end of that telephone line? What was happening?

Gran was about to ask all these questions, and maybe answer the one about where he got his brass C, when he heard a rumbling. Then he felt it. It sounded and felt much like the rumbling he'd heard and felt before, when he'd been chased by the hurricane, but this time it was louder, and he was sure it was moving far quicker. He looked to Catalina, who was listening intently, her eyes closed.

"I had a feeling this might happen," Catalina said, her eyes still closed. "We'll have to get a move on." But she made no movement. She seemed to be deliberating.

"Is it the Hollows?" Gran asked.

Catalina didn't answer. She lifted a finger, telling him to shush and wait. He stood, silent and ready.

Finally she opened her eyes, gave him her look, and he knew: Of course it was the Hollows. Her eyes closed again, as if she needed to block out all unnecessary senses to concentrate on what her ears were telling her. She opened her eyes once more, and this time she seemed ready for action.

"I think they're taking an interest in you," she said. "We have to get to the surface."

The howling sound of the Hollows was growing louder.

"So let's go!" Gran said.

"We will. I'm just trying to figure out the best way up."

Catalina stood, her hands on her head as if she were suffering a terrible migraine. Finally she nodded to herself and started running.

She was fast. She was twenty feet away before she thought to turn around and yell, "Follow me!"

Chapter SIXTY-SIX

They ran down a long tunnel, dodging the supports all the way. Now the rumbling was deafening. Soon the tunnel split into two. Catalina took the leftward path.

Gran followed, and had the momentary thought that the Hollows would be tricked down the rightward path, but in seconds he heard the wind behind him. The walls of the tunnel began to shake.

"It's coming!" he yelled ahead to Catalina. She said nothing. Of course she knew this.

This leftward path angled upward, and the going became increasingly difficult. It was like running up a slippery ramp. Then the tunnel got steeper and running up it was like scampering up a playground slide greased with oil. Ahead, Catalina had slowed, but she

was making her way up with great agility. She was using her legs and her hands in a spidery way, moving so quickly that she seemed to be barely touching the surface of the tunnel.

The wind was so loud now, and so close, that Gran couldn't hear anything but the howling, the scraping of all the stones and dirt the wind carried with it.

"Wait!" Gran yelled, but Catalina made no effort to slow down.

Finally she stopped and, her legs splayed out as if she were a gymnast doing the splits, she removed the handle from her waist and thrust it into the wall of the tunnel. A door appeared and Gran saw the welcome sight of a night sky, framed in a rectangle. But he was twenty feet below.

"Get up here!" she yelled.

Gran looked up. He tried to find a foothold or a handhold and saw nothing. How had Catalina gotten that high?

The roar of the Hollows grew louder. The first rocks hurtled forth from the maelstrom and landed at Gran's feet. He had no options. And just as he'd had the sense before that the wind was a thinking thing, and he intuitively knew its plans, now he knew that it did not intend to tunnel through the Earth. This time, he was sure, the Hollows were coming for him. He was sure that they would take him and retreat with him, as a ravenous lion would with its prey.

And he had no way to save himself.

He jumped, he screamed, he grabbed at the walls of the tunnel. His hands were useless, his feet had no function. Pain radiated from his shoulder. His face was soaked with tears and Catalina had abandoned him.

But then she hadn't after all. He felt a snaky thing on his shoulder, and turned to find it was a rope.

"Grab it!" she yelled from above. He looked up to find her face framed by the new door.

With his good arm, he grabbed the rope.

The Hollows came for him with a new speed and vengeance. They came like ten caged, rabid dogs suddenly unleashed.

"I can't pull you without your help," Catalina yelled. "Climb!"

Gran scrambled up the rough dirt wall, his shoulder screaming as Catalina pulled. Soon he was up and out. Catalina closed the door with finality and threw herself back on the ground, exhausted.

Chapter **SIXTY-SEVEN**

Gran lay under the welcome dark sky, gasping for air. He was filthy and soaked in sweat. He didn't recognize the part of town where they'd emerged, though he could hear the sound of the river. In the distance, he could see the lights of the town.

"I don't understand what's happening."

These were the words Gran wanted to say, but Catalina had just said them instead. This left Gran doubly baffled. If Catalina didn't understand, then who did?

"You're okay?" she asked him. Or rather, she declared it: "You're okay." Gran saw her look him over, as if she could discern, just by scanning him, the presence of broken limbs or injured organs. Satisfied, she walked off. "See ya," she said over her shoulder.

Gran crawled to his feet, stumbled toward her and finally caught up with her. "You mean you don't understand why it's happening now, or where it's happening, or . . ."

Catalina sped up, as if wanting to outpace Gran, to leave him behind—the same way Gran sometimes did with Maisie.

"Catalina," he said. "Please."

She exhaled loudly. "I just mean there's something new," she said. "From what I was told when I started, it used to be that these incidents would happen once every few years at most—and you never saw a whole house disappear. It never got that bad. It used to be that I'd get an occasional call that there was a new tunnel, and I'd go down and prop it up and that would be that. But now it's happening all the time. The Hollows are everywhere now. That's why the Regional Manager is so interested."

"So that was the Regional Manager?"

"What was?"

"On the phone. The person who called on the phone."

"I wasn't on the phone. And there's no such thing as the Regional Manager."

"You just said there was."

"No I didn't."

Gran didn't feel like arguing the point. Catalina didn't seem to be able to decide on what information she could reveal and what she had to conceal.

"So the Hollows happen other places, too?" he asked.

"You think this is the only town with sadness?"

The town came into view below. Catalina paused, as if unsure that she wanted to rejoin the people of Carousel. From their vantage point, they could see that City Hall was still brightly lit. A crowd of people was outside.

"What do you mean?" Gran asked. "That's what makes the Hollows come?"

"You know sharks?" she asked.

"Like, personally?"

"No. But you've heard of sharks, right? You've seen pictures of them, watched them on TV?"

"Sure," Gran said.

"You know how they sense blood in the water and then come to feed?"

"Yes."

"Well, this is the same thing. Only instead of sharks, it's this voracious underground hurricane that thinks and feels, and tunnels through the earth. And instead of blood in the water that attracts them, it's despair, emptiness, hopelessness."

"I don't get it. They're attracted to despair?"

"That's as much as we can figure out. The Hollows sense it and come to make it worse. Like the shark—it comes when something's bleeding and then finishes the job."

"And the wind thinks?"

"You saw it. Don't you think it thinks?"

"I guess so. It seemed to have a plan."

"It does have a plan."

"What *is* the plan?"

"I don't know yet."

Gran and Catalina stood for a second, both of them thinking about all the things they did not know.

"So we just wait for the next collapse?" Gran asked.

Catalina's face darkened. "No. We wait for the next new tunnel and go down and prop it up as long as we can. Actually, I go down there alone and prop it up. Not you. You're done. You're out. The Regional Manager doesn't want you involved."

"So there *is* a Regional Manager!" Gran said.

"Maybe," Catalina admitted.

"Why can't I be a Lifter?" he asked.

"Because this work is dangerous and you're not a Lifter."

"I know it's dangerous. And that's fine with me. So how do I become a Lifter?"

"That's up to the Regional Manager."

"So do you apply or something?"

"Do you apply? No, you don't apply. This isn't a job at Burger King. Boy, he'd laugh at that one."

"Okay, then how?"

"You're called."

"How do you get called?"

Catalina stopped and looked into Gran's eyes. Or rather, she looked at his forehead, and spoke directly to his forehead. (This is what people often do when delivering bad news: they speak to your forehead.) "Listen," she said. "You already know more than you should. Can we just let it go? You should get home. Just go back to your perfect little life. This work is for people who know about mess. Who aren't afraid of mess."

"Perfect life?" Gran said, almost laughing. "Are you kidding?

 And I already figured out how to get underground. I did it with my own handle."

"It's called a Lift," Catalina said.

"What is? This handle?"

Catalina pointed to Gran's handle, and to her own. "These are called Lifts," she said. "When they create doors in the earth, they're called Lifts. Capital *L*. Not handles, lowercase *h*. Got it?"

"Fine," Gran said.

"And that thing in your hand isn't a Lift. You just followed me. That thing didn't open any door."

"Yes it did. My great-great-grandfather made this." Gran was convinced that the fact that his ancestor had made it, had hammered its shape and carved it by hand, and was from this town, had something to do with it working.

"It's not possible," Catalina said. "You have to be a Lifter to use a

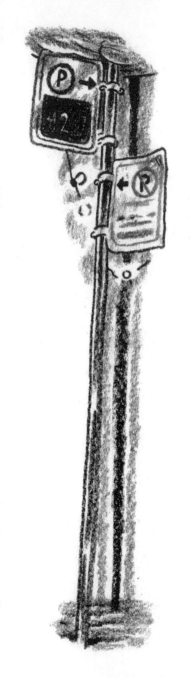

Lift, and you're not a Lifter. So you can't come. You really should go home and watch TV or something. Play a game. This Hollows business will only get nastier and weirder and more treacherous. That's what the Regional Manager says. Get out while you can. I have to go back to work. And you need to go home. Take your nice watch and go back to bed."

"I won't. I'm staying. I'll be a Lifter too."

For a second something passed over Catalina's face. It was almost as if she was impressed. Then she shook it off.

And with that, she dropped onto one knee, inserted her handle into the ground, pulled open a door, and dropped in. She closed the door so quickly Gran didn't even have a chance.

Chapter SIXTY-EIGHT

Gran had a problem, and that was that whenever someone said nasty things to him, as Catalina just had, he collapsed. It had happened to him before, just about every month since he was five. Some classmate would call him short, or strange, or poor, or Granite Countertop, and though he had seen films where a boy or girl was called names, and they pressed on and overcame these judgments, he found himself unable to do so. When he was treated cruelly, especially by someone he liked and admired, someone like Catalina Catalan, he felt himself drop like a marionette whose strings have been cut.

He stood there, looking at the invisible door through which Catalina had just disappeared, and his eyes felt raw. His throat was dry. He felt like he'd just lost the only friend he had in the world.

But had Catalina ever really been his friend?

Probably not. She'd helped him once. And then she'd asked for his help, and asked him to borrow his mother's wheelchair. Would a friend do that? He wasn't sure.

He was sure, though, that now he didn't want to be around Catalina Catalan. She was mean. He wanted to be anywhere but with her. He was filled with a sudden anger toward her, a cleansing anger.

So he went home. He walked down the hill, through the trees, and through the park until he reached City Hall. The lights he'd seen from above were burning bright, and the lawn was full of people. They were arguing outside, and the voices from inside were loud, too. Some people carried Propositions P&S signs, and others held Propositions M&H placards. One woman supporting P&S was dressed as a tree. A man supporting M&H was wearing a moose costume.

Gran walked on. He wanted to be home.

When he saw the yellow lights through the windows, he cried, just a little. Maybe what he did wasn't actually crying. His throat simply closed and his breath climbed quickly and sunk again, and his eyes were a little wetter than usual. But he didn't cry. No water left his eyes. No one could call it crying.

He dropped his Lift behind a bush in the yard and opened the front door. Maisie was there, in the foyer. It was late, but Maisie was still awake. All rules of the house had been thrown away, it seemed.

"Oh you should have seen it!" she said, and pointed to the TV. "There was this horse, and every time it wanted something, it nodded like a real person, and then it learned how to talk by watching TV, but it had this crazy voice!"

Gran wasn't sure he'd ever heard Maisie talk so much all at once. He followed her to the living room, where she pointed again to the screen, even though by now the horse show was gone and the news was on.

Gran dropped into the soft couch and brought Maisie up onto his lap. He held her tight and smelled her strawberry-scented hair.

"What are you doing?" Maisie asked, squirming away from him.

All Gran wanted to do was sit with her, close to her warmth, her squirmy arms and legs, to hear her ridiculous cartoon voice, and to stay home, and be away from the chaos underground. He didn't need to be contending with underground hurricanes hellbent on hurt; he didn't

need to be contending with Catalina. He was happy to be home, and safe, and he could smell something good coming from the kitchen.

"Whoa," Maisie said. "Look."

She pointed to the TV, where video taken from a helicopter was showing what seemed to be a giant sinkhole.

"Turn it up," Gran said, and Maisie adjusted the volume.

A reporter stood in front of a chaotic scene—fire engines, police cars and dozens of rescue workers. "I'm here in Buenos Aires, Argentina, and as you can see, there's a swarm of activity here as authorities and workers try to find survivors of the collapse . . ."

"Dinner!" Gran's mom announced from the kitchen. Gran, in a daze from his encounter with the Hollows and now the knowledge that the winds were still at work and seemed to be expanding their range, sat down and stared at his food. In his altered state, it didn't look like food at all. The baked beans looked like a cave, the celery looked like supports needed to hold the ceiling up.

Just as Gran's mother rolled to the table to start on her own dinner, her phone rang. She looked at her screen, and then put the phone on the table and turned it to speaker.

"We're all here!" she said.

Gran and Maisie said hello to their father.

"Hi, you two," he said, sounding weary. "Can you ask your mother to turn off the speakerphone? I have something to talk to her about."

Gran knew that usually his mother was careful not to have adult

conversations in front of him and Maisie.
Countless times she had cut a discussion
short, to be continued later, in his parents'
bedroom. So it was unsettling when she
continued this conversation, sitting at the
table in front of him and Maisie.

"What do you want me to tell the
kids?" she asked.

Gran and Maisie could hear nothing
on the other end of the line.

"That doesn't help," she said.

Silence. Gran looked over to Maisie.
Typically she wasn't tuned in to the
parental frequency—she never seemed to
hear any of their fighting. But this time,
she was staring straight at their mother,
rapt and comprehending.

"So what—you're not back for Thanks-
giving, Christmas?" Gran's mom said.

Silence.

"Wait. I was kidding. You're serious?"
Silence.

"I'm getting very tired talking to you.
I'm hanging up."

Gran's mother always did exactly what

she said she would do. All his life, Gran knew this to be true. If she said she would pick Gran up at five o'clock, she was there precisely at five. If she said she was about to hang up the phone, she hung up.

Gran's father, though, sometimes had a more slippery grasp of time and promises. He had told Gran that he could go to sleepaway camp last summer, but when June arrived, he said there was no way he could go, that the prices for those camps were ridiculous, that he had never promised Gran a sleepaway camp.

But Gran knew he had promised.

And the last night he'd been at home, he'd said that Gran and Maisie could get dessert if they ate their dinners, but when they finished, he said that they didn't need dessert. *"Need" has nothing to do with it,* Gran wanted to say. *"Need" wasn't the point. The point was you promised.*

And here your narrator would like to agree with Gran. A promise is like the earth underneath us. It must be solid. How can we walk, and run, and live and laugh, when we can't count on the ground beneath us? And so it is with promises. They keep us upright. They hold up everyone and everything.

Chapter **SIXTY-NINE**

The next day, Carousel Middle School was in a state of elevated distress. When Gran entered, he found that the sinkhole had grown. Now there was only a narrow catwalk from the front door to the hallways where the classrooms were. Everything in the front foyer had fallen in.

When Gran entered the Duke's office for lunch, he found him standing, his back turned to Gran and his shoulders pressed to the cinder-block wall. He was talking heatedly, but there was no one else in the room. For a second Gran thought the Duke had lost his mind and was talking to the Earth balls stacked at the back of the room.

Finally the Duke turned around, and his eyes widened when he saw Gran. Gran realized the Duke was on the telephone. He held a large black receiver in his hand, its long spiral cord dangling on the ground.

"We have to do what we can," the Duke said, and hung up. He stepped toward Gran. "Gran, how are you, my friend?" He looked at his watch. "You're early, or I'm late."

Gran looked at his watch. He was right on time. He'd been coming to the Duke's office every day, at the same time, for a week at least.

"I'm sorry," the Duke said. "You're probably on time. Things have just been busy around here, with the sinkhole and all. You hungry?"

The Duke put a record on, and the music overtook the room. The Duke relaxed, and Gran did too, and when they were done eating, the Duke exhaled loudly. He was sitting on the couch and leaned toward Gran, who was sitting on a folding chair across from him.

"You seem sad," he said.

Gran shrugged.

"Is it about what's happening at school?" the Duke asked.

"Not really," Gran said.

"Something at home?"

"I don't know," Gran said.

The Duke leaned back and looked at the ceiling. "My mom and dad used to fight. Maybe once a week, they'd argue to the point where my sisters and I had to leave. My parents made us stay upstairs while they fought, so we crawled out onto the roof and climbed down the latticework on the side of the house. We'd go to the river. You know the river, in the middle of town?"

Gran nodded.

"We'd throw sticks in the water for an hour or so, and then come home."

The Duke brought his eyes back to Gran, and they were wet. "I don't know if that helps you at all. But I know that at your age, you can feel powerless. And the powerlessness can make you angry."

Seeing tears in the Duke's eyes, and knowing how right he was about what Gran was feeling, Gran almost cried himself. But instead he got up quickly.

"I have to go," he said, and left.

Chapter **SEVENTY**

G ran sleepwalked through the rest of the day, and at home, he went straight to his room and stayed there until he fell asleep. His mother didn't wake him up for dinner.

"You looked like you needed the rest," she told him the next morning.

"You were talking a lot in your sleep," Maisie said. "And kicking. And you punched your pillow. And who's Catalina? You said her name a bunch of times."

Catalina wasn't at school that day. Not that Gran could see, at least, and that was just as well. He avoided the Duke too, though his feelings about the Duke were complicated. He wasn't mad at the

Duke, but Gran didn't feel like talking about whatever the Duke wanted to talk about.

For the first time since Gran had come to Carousel Middle School, he joined the boys in the circle at lunch, and he stood while a boy ran from the other side, leapt, and kicked him in the chest. It hurt, but not as much as Gran had expected. Then it was his turn. He ran from his side of the circle to the boy opposite him, jumped, and kicked him in the chest. It felt good, but not as good as Gran had hoped.

Chapter SEVENTY-ONE

The next day, where the kicking circle had been, there was a hole. A hole the exact circumference of the kicking circle. Gran arrived at school to find half the school circling the gaping chasm.

"Okay, show's over," Ms. Rhapsod said. She herded the kids away from the hole and into the school.

"My class, follow me," she said. "We're having a special program today." Gran and the rest of his class followed her into the library and to the grid of study carrels at the back of the room. "Everyone take a desk."

The carrels, a grid of cubicles, each built for one student to work on one computer, were an oddly comfortable place for Gran. There,

he couldn't be seen, and he could relax and work on lessons at his own pace.

Ms. Rhapsod went on: "The administration here at school is aware that recent developments involving gaping sinkholes and collapsing buildings might be troubling for some of you. So the school will be offering counseling to all students. Of course, due to budget cuts, we have no school counselor, so the district has provided us with an automated counseling system that you'll be using today."

Gran and the other students put on headsets that were attached to each cubicle. Each headset had a microphone on a cord that connected to the desk.

"This will be our morning," Ms. Rhapsod said. "You'll stay and be counseled by the machine until lunch. No getting up. No monkey business. Okay? Okay. Commence counseling."

"Greetings, student," a woman's voice said through Gran's headphones. It seemed to be a recording of an actual woman, as opposed to a robotic voice. The recorded voice explained that she would be offering 340 questions, and the answers provided by the listener would determine the direction of the questions that followed. "By the end of our session, I am confident that our conversation will help you . . ." there was a long pause, as if the computer was attaching the appropriate end to the sentence, ". . . cope with this difficult time."

Gran waited for the first question, but realized the first thing he needed to cope with was his bladder. He needed to pee. He raised his hand.

Ms. Rhapsod shot him a sharp look and shook her head. She pointed to the headphones.

"How are you feeling today?" the voice in the headset said.

Gran answered, "Fine."

"That's good to hear," the voice said. "Have you been troubled by . . ." again there was a pause as the computer sorted through possible ends to the question, ". . . recent events at your school or town?"

"No," Gran said.

His bladder roared. He pushed his legs together. He could hold it. He was twelve years old. Of course he could hold it. If he got through the automated questions quickly enough, he might be allowed to leave class early.

"Have you found yourself unable to concentrate in school?" the voice said.

"No," Gran answered.

"I'm noticing that your answers are monosyllabic," the voice said. "This can be a sign of depression. Do you think you are depressed?"

Gran was stuck. The answer was no, he didn't feel depressed, but he couldn't answer with one word.

"I feel happy," he said.

"What's that? I didn't catch it," the voice said.

"I feel happy," he repeated.

"What's that? I didn't catch it," the voice said.

The automated system didn't seem to be able to recognize this sentence. Gran tried another way of saying it.

"I'm okay."

"I think I heard you say 'I'm okay.' Is that correct?"

"Yes," he said.

"Hm," the voice said, as if both disappointed and concerned. "I'm noticing that your answers are monosyllabic," she said again. "This can be a sign of depression. Do you think you are depressed?"

"I feel happy," he said again.

"Great. Happiness is a positive sign," the voice said. "But sometimes happiness can also mask sadness. Especially when you are dealing with . . . recent events at your school or town."

By now Gran's bladder was screaming. He didn't know how the

system counted its questions—did "What's that? I didn't catch it" count as a question?—but he was sure he hadn't made it far. As far as he could tell, he'd answered four. He raised his hand again. Again Ms. Rhapsod shot him a terrifying look. He lowered his hand.

"Sometimes events around us seem out of our control, and that's okay," the voice said. "You are a young person, and very little is within your control. You must release yourself from responsibility for these things and acknowledge your powerlessness to affect the adult world around you. Do you think you can do that?"

Gran didn't know what to answer. Again trying to avoid one-word answers, he said, "I believe I can."

"Did I hear you say 'I play kick the can'?" the voice said.

This went on far longer than Gran's bladder could hold back the tide. Somewhere in the middle of the session, Gran felt a warm fluid streaming down his leg. Even though he knew this might happen, when it did, there was a brief moment when he imagined it might be a flood overtaking the school. But he knew this was not the case. He knew it was his own doing. He was wetting his pants. And he couldn't stop. He had no chance to make it to the bathroom in time to finish. He could only wait it out. Which he did, calmly, until he realized he was wearing khaki pants, and they would darken tragically.

Chapter **SEVENTY-TWO**

At the end of the morning, after Gran and his soaked khakis had answered 340 questions from the automated counseling service, he watched as his classmates began to stand up.

All he needed to do was wait for them all to leave and then he'd race to the bathroom, or to the Duke's office, or home. Anything. But then Ms. Rhapsod spoke.

"The counseling system has determined it best for the whole class to eat lunch together, as a bonding exercise. So let's line up at the door."

Gran's cubicle was in the darkest corner of the library, so he thought he had a chance of hiding and avoiding notice. After all, Ms. Rhapsod hadn't said his name since the day of the nicknames.

He kept his head low and listened to the movement of the class toward the door. In thirty seconds they would be gone. He counted to ten. Twenty.

"Who's missing?" Ms. Rhapsod asked loudly.

"No one," a student said. Gran knew this was the voice of Emma Thewlis, who sat in the front of the room and acted as a kind of assistant to Ms. Rhapsod.

"We have twenty-two students," Ms. Rhapsod said. "And there are twenty-one lined up. Someone's missing."

Under normal circumstances, having the entire class unable to identify him as the missing student would have been upsetting, but at that moment, Gran's invisibility gave him hope. He heard shuffling near the door, and was sure the class had left the library. He exhaled.

"Here he is!" a voice boomed from just behind him. He startled. It was Ms. Rhapsod. Her hand was now on his head, as if he were a carrot she was about to pick.

"Get up," she said. "Alacrity, alacrity."

"I can't," he said.

Gran decided he would appeal to the sympathy of this teacher: if she saw that he'd wet his pants, she would understand his need to wait till his classmates were gone. She would nod, would put her hand on his shoulder, say that she understood, and allow him to sneak away to the bathroom, to the nurse's office, somewhere. So he pushed his chair back to reveal to her his soaked lap and leg. It was the first time he was seeing the damage himself. It was far more extensive than he'd imagined.

"What happened?" she asked, far too loudly.

"Nothing," he whispered, and gestured to his lap again, making a downward gesture, to indicate the flow of water down to his shoes. He didn't know how else to get her to understand what had happened. Wasn't she a teacher? Shouldn't she know something about situations like this?

"Okay, if it's nothing," she said, "then line up at the door. Before I have to give you a check."

The checks were her system of demerits. Notice of each and every check was emailed to the student's parents. Three checks in any given week meant you were sent to Mr. Juan, who was the school's behavioral expert.

He knew his mother would be devastated by even one check, and she had had enough to deal with recently.

He stood.

"Alacrity!" Ms. Rhapsod said, and strode to the line at the door. Gran's mind raced for a plan.

"Can I use the bathroom before lunch?" he asked.

"No, we're already late," she said.

He followed her to the line, staying directly behind her so the other students wouldn't see what he'd done to his khakis.

It worked. It worked in part because he was hidden behind Ms. Rhapsod, and in part because none of the other students in the class were watching them approach. They weren't the least bit interested in Gran, or where Gran was, or whether or not Gran had been found. They were ready for lunch.

So the line made its way down the hallway, past the sinkhole, and toward the cafeteria. Gran could see the double doors ahead, and knew that once he entered, anything could happen. Ms. Rhapsod would peel off and head to the teachers' table, or return to the teachers' lounge. She could offer no more protection.

And when she peeled off, the 380 kids in the cafeteria would see that Gran had wet his pants.

Then he had an idea.

If he could get himself to the trays, then he could slide himself down the cafeteria line, with his front facing away from the tables and kids. And then, in a stroke of brilliance, he had a second idea. If he could make it to the fridge containing the milk, then he could get a milk out and open it.

And spill it all over himself.

And if he could spill it all over himself, the darkness all over his khakis would look like milk, not urine. And anyone could spill milk. Everyone did spill milk.

And that is how it happened.

Ms. Rhapsod peeled off. Gran rushed to the trays, pushing himself against the rails. He looked around. No one had seen him. He put a bowl of chili on his tray. He got a side salad. And then he grabbed two milks, opened one—as if he was so thirsty for

2 percent he couldn't wait—and made a show of spilling it all over his pants.

"Aw man!" he roared.

Because he was near invisible, not a lot of people cared. He heard someone say "Smooth!" and someone else giggle, but that was it. He grabbed some napkins, dried his legs a bit, and then, at the closest table, he sat down with his tray.

He felt pretty proud of himself. No one, it seemed, had noticed. He sat there, eating his chili—because he wanted to act so casual that even with a wet lap he couldn't be torn away from his delicious lunch—and while he ate, he actually did feel pretty good. He had pulled off a fairly ludicrous plan to disguise a truly horrific mishap. It had worked. All was reset to zero. To neutral.

He sat, eating his chili with great nonchalance, occasionally sweeping his eyes around the room to be sure no one was secretly laughing at him. He saw no one looking his way. No one cared.

But then he saw one pair of eyes watching him. They were tilted in amusement, and the mouth below these eyes was set in a smirk.

It was Catalina Catalan.

He looked down. His neck burned, his face burned, sweat soaked his armpits. There was no part of the skin covering his body that was not in some state of change. His legs were still wet. His whole torso was marshy with sweat. And his face and neck were on fire.

He looked up again, hoping Catalina was looking away, that she didn't really care so much about what she'd seen, but her eyes were still upon him, the smirk still a laughing stripe across her oval face. He wanted to leave, but knew he couldn't. Or shouldn't. He'd just barely gotten away with the ruse of the spilled milk, and if he left the cafeteria early, with his pants still wet, he'd risk attracting attention.

So he sat, avoiding Catalina's eyes, avoiding everyone's eyes, and he finished his lunch and waited for his khakis to dry, hoping they would dry in a way that didn't reveal what was now a combination of urine and milk. What kind of stain would that produce? He hoped for the best.

Chapter SEVENTY-THREE

When lunch ended, Gran waited till the last person left the room, then got up, carrying his tray below his waist, hiding his lap and legs, and brought it to the trash and recycling area. The trash can was near the door, and the door was not far from the hall bathroom, so if he could make it to the door, and then to the bathroom, he could finish the job of drying himself.

He bussed his tray, put it back in the rack, and made it out the door. He was a few feet from the bathroom when he felt a plaid shadow nearby.

"That was good," she said.

It was Catalina. She'd been waiting. Gran assumed she'd seen him spill the milk. He didn't mind that. As long as she hadn't seen the whole thing—

"I watched the whole thing," she said. "I saw you come in with your wet khakis." She winked, as if she were in on a secret. "Then I saw you spill the milk on purpose. I liked how you sat down all quick-like. And how you waited till the last kid left the cafeteria. All of that was very clever."

Gran felt sick. He wasn't sure he could stand up for much longer. He wanted to get away from her, from the school.

"My respect for you just went up ten points, Gran. Maybe twenty," she said. "That showed some seriously innovative thinking on the fly. Where are you going?"

Gran was trying to run, to get to the bathroom, but something was holding him back. He realized it was Catalina. She was holding him by the shirt.

"Let go please," he said.

"I'm sorry I called you names the other night," she said.

"Fine." He tried to escape, to no avail. She was strong.

"I just thought you were some rich kid."

"Okay," he said, and again tried to leave. She was very strong, and she kept talking.

"I saw your fancy watch," she went on, "and I made assumptions."

Gran paused in his struggle to escape. This was interesting to him. This was the first time anyone had made an assumption like that about him. People had always assumed he was shy, or unathletic, or poor, but they had never assumed, looking at the old watch his father had given him, that he was wealthy. He almost felt good about it.

"Listen," she said. "I actually need your help." There was something softer about her tone, her eyes, now, and he took the opportunity to yank himself free.

He ran to the boys' bathroom, ducked into a stall and closed the door. He needed to be alone, finally, to fix his pants. But he realized he was not alone.

Catalina had followed him. He could see her dirty boots under the stall door.

"You're not supposed to be in here," Gran said.

"I'll wait till you're done," she said. "Didn't you just pee all over your pants? How can you be peeing again?"

"No," he said. "I'm not . . . Just. Please go. Can I meet you outside?"

"There's not much time," Catalina said. "A lot's happening. You saw how the school's falling into the earth. There's activity all over town, and the Regional Manager's all over me. And tonight's the big Proposition meeting at City Hall. Then I've got to—" She stopped, as if catching herself before saying too much. "Anyway. I can't handle it all myself."

Gran was torn.

"You can do something about all this. You'll feel useful, as opposed to just sitting in a carrel wetting your pants."

"You're mean," Gran said.

"Sorry," Catalina said. "I don't mean to be. I tend to think I'm funny, but I know it comes off as mean. But I like you. And I think you're actually someone who wants to do something to help around here. I think you're powerful."

Gran had never been called powerful before. It felt strange and good.

"Will you come with me?" she asked.

Chapter **SEVENTY-FOUR**

This was the first time in his life Gran had missed school. In all his life he'd never missed a day. Never an hour. And now he was leaving school, in the middle of school. In fact, he was leaving school *through* the middle of school—through the sinkhole that had swallowed most of the main foyer.

"It's the easiest way in," Catalina said.

They waited until the bell rang, and jumped in.

When they landed in a heap, Gran saw only a jumble of tiles and rocks, paper and folders and pencils. Catalina saw the tunnel through which the Hollows had come.

"Let's go!" she whispered.

He followed her into the darkness.

"What's the rush?" he asked.

"The vote on Propositions M&H and P&S is tonight. At City Hall."

"I know. My mom's going."

"Well, that makes it worse. The building's going to be full of people, and it's already tilting."

The tunnel widened and Catalina began to run. Gran followed, ducking and weaving as the tunnel bent left and right, rose and fell.

When they arrived, Gran stopped cold.

Before him was a wild tangle of tunnels, some small, some large, a thicket of entwined and crisscrossing tubes— and every one of them was vibrating.

"Wait!" he yelled. "It's too late."

The earth everywhere around them was rumbling and shaking. Dirt was falling from the tunnel roofs.

"It's not too late," Catalina said. "Just get to work."

Chapter **SEVENTY-FIVE**

Gran got to work helping Catalina, and they labored steadily through the afternoon. They'd never worked so hard or so long. Soon it was five o'clock, then six, and Gran's shoulder throbbed. But with every pole they installed, the shaking from above decreased. The tunnels were stabilizing.

By early evening, Gran and Catalina were working in different parts of the tunnels, and while he was using tree trunks and scrap metal, he noticed that the supports Catalina was using were strangely uniform. They were poles, each about six inches across, all of them smooth and striped by flecks of gold paint.

"Where'd you get these?" Gran asked.

"They were already here," she said. "There might be a few more down that way if you need 'em." She pointed down a wide tunnel that seemed to lead directly under the front lawn of City Hall. Gran followed the tunnel until he saw, emerging from the tunnel walls, a few fragments of the same kind of once-golden poles.

Gran gasped. Instantly it came together. The poles were from the carousel the Duke had been talking about. He was sure of it. The carousel had been swallowed by the first sinkhole, and that had been here. It had to be.

Gran dug into the tunnel wall, looking for a horse or zebra.

"What are you doing?" Catalina yelled from afar. "Get back here and help me."

Gran grabbed the poles he could carry and rushed to her.

"What were you doing?" she asked.

"I'll tell you after," he said.

They installed the last of the poles in the most vulnerable parts of the tunnel system, and stood back to assess their work.

"I don't know," Catalina said. "These are strong, but there's a lot of weight above."

"What happens if . . ." For the first time, Gran thought about the possibility of getting stuck in the tunnels, or worse, crushed under the weight of all that dirt.

"It's never happened," Catalina said. "If we feel like it's collapsing, we can use this to go down." She held out her Lift. "Or up. There's always time."

Just then, the earth around them shook, as if to contradict her. Behind them, there was a loud crack. They turned to see that one of the golden poles had snapped in half. The tunnel ceiling above it sagged dramatically.

"Haven't seen *that* happen in a while," Catalina said. "And we're out of supports." Her eyes darted around for options. "The meeting at City Hall starts in an hour," she said, "but we've done all we can do."

"Wait," Gran said. The fragments of the City Hall carousel had brought the Duke to mind, and the Duke, indirectly, had given Gran a plan.

"Give me twenty minutes," he said.

Chapter **SEVENTY-SIX**

There are times when humans fly. Our feet still touch the ground, but only slightly, as we run so fast we are really more like herons skimming the water as they take flight.

And when we are flying we feel happy, and we feel purposeful, and we feel most like ourselves, especially when we are flying this way with an urgent task to do.

Gran's urgent task was to reach the Duke's office, and he did so in minutes. But he found the door locked. Gran looked at his watch. It was 7:32. Of course the Duke wouldn't be at school so late. But why was the door locked? It had never been locked before.

Gran cursed his own stupidity. He'd left Catalina for nothing. He'd have to return empty-handed. He thumped his head on the door. Then his head began sliding. The door was moving.

"Grant?"

It was the Duke. He was wearing a bathrobe. "Just . . . uh, cleaning up some things in here," he said. "And doing some filing. This is the robe I like to use when I'm filing."

Gran looked inside, and saw no sign that the Duke had been doing any filing. He did see a towel by the sink, and on the coffee table in front of the couch there was evidence of a half-eaten grilled cheese sandwich. At one end of the couch, the same couch where Gran had been eating his lunch the past few weeks, there was a bedpillow. If Gran didn't know better, he would think that the Duke was living in the storage space.

"Why are you here?" the Duke asked.

Gran snapped out of his reverie.

"I need those," he said, pointing to the back of the room.

Chapter **SEVENTY-SEVEN**

"I'm happy to help you, but this is unusual," the Duke said. "I'm sure this is the first time a student has asked to borrow all my Earth balls after dark. Come to think of it, this is the first time in thirty years a student has asked to borrow them at all. You sure you can't tell me why you need them?"

"Do you trust me that it's important?" Gran said.

"I trust you always, Grant."

"So can I have them?"

"Are you sure you don't want hockey sticks? I have some you can use."

Gran paused for a second. "No, the Earth balls are better."

The Duke cleared a path for the Earth balls. "Where are we bringing them?" he asked.

"I can't tell you," Gran said.

The Duke might have been annoyed. Gran had disturbed his nighttime routine and asked him to help move Earth balls—they were not light!—and all the while, he was being kept in the dark about why and where they were going. But the Duke seemed cheerful, and not so concerned with the particulars of Gran's plan.

In fact, after all the balls were out of the storage room and in the hallway, the Duke produced a wagon, like a Radio Flyer but far bigger. "This should help," he said.

They loaded the balls onto the wagon, and made it outside. Gran was ready to turn and pull the wagon down the road and into the tunnels when the Duke cleared his throat. He was holding a bicycle pump.

"You probably need this."

Chapter SEVENTY-EIGHT

When Gran reached the tunnel under City Hall, he didn't see Catalina. And it was clear more tunnels had buckled or collapsed. He feared the worst—that she'd gotten stuck.

"You were gone too long," she said. Gran wheeled around to find her. He'd never been so glad to be scolded.

"What are those?" she said, pointing at the deflated Earth balls he'd pulled into the tunnel. "And why do you have a bike pump? Have you lost your mind?"

"Watch," he said, and dragged the ball over to a portion of the tunnel that was sagging badly.

He pumped quickly, and together they watched the Earth ball

inflate. It grew to three feet tall, then four, then five. It filled the tunnel almost completely.

Gran smiled, very proud of himself, and looked to see that Catalina's face had been tempted into the tiniest smile, too. It was a good moment, and Gran felt like he truly had Catalina's respect.

Then the ceiling fell.

Chapter **SEVENTY-NINE**

Not entirely. It dropped suddenly, but the Earth ball had saved her—had saved both of them.

"You okay?" Gran asked.

He knelt next to Catalina, who had been knocked to the ground.

"I'm okay," she said, rubbing her head, which was brown with dirt. "How are we not dead?" She didn't wait for an answer. "You have more of those?"

The ball was bigger and easier to manipulate than their usual crosshatched poles and beams, and it covered far more space.

"I have twelve," he said.

"Wait," she said. "Did you get these from that storage guy's place at school?"

"I did. How did you know?"

"I go to school there too. I've been there a lot longer than you, remember."

"I know. Sorry."

"You're not so fancy just because you brought some giant volleyballs."

"Whatever you say," Gran said.

For a long few seconds Catalina stared Gran down, and he didn't blink. She made a tiny sound that acknowledged that he wasn't backing down, and that she was just a little impressed.

Then they got started. Catalina moved each Earth ball into position in the most vulnerable parts of the tunnel system under City Hall, and one by one, Gran pumped each to its full size.

The only problem with the Earth balls was that they so completely filled the tunnels that Gran and Catalina had to be strategic about where they put them, and where they put themselves. Otherwise they would get stuck on the wrong side of one of the balls, and would have no way to get back.

"Wait," Catalina said. "Hear that?"

Chapter **EIGHTY**

Gran knew the sound. It was the hoarse and maniacal wheezing of the Hollows. They were coming.

"What do we do?" he asked Catalina.

She had her ear to the earthen wall, listening intently.

"We wait and see if the Earth balls hold. The Hollows sense that something here hasn't gone to plan. They thought City Hall would have collapsed by now, but it's still standing. Now they're coming back to finish the job."

Catalina listened silently to the vibrations.

"Sounds like they're coming from another direction. Let's wait here."

"We can't wait here," Gran said. "What if they—"

Catalina finished his sentence. "What if they pop those balls like balloons?" She thought for a second, and answered matter-of-factly. "Then we'll have to try to escape before they get us, or City Hall collapses on us with everyone in it. Or both."

Again she put her ear to the tunnel wall. "They're really close now. Listen."

Catalina gestured for Gran to put his ear to the earth. He did, and was surprised at how clearly he could hear the approaching Hollows. They sounded like a roomful of whispers, the voices arguing and growing louder. He'd always wondered how Catalina understood them, but now that he'd encountered the Hollows up close, it was as if he'd learned their language and could discern their movements and intentions.

He heard the winds approach, howling and angry, as if they were annoyed they had to return to a job they'd considered finished. Then the snarling wind seemed to slow, perplexed. Gran felt sure that the Hollows had encountered one of the Earth balls, and were baffled by what they were facing.

Gran heard the wind back up, and retreat, then re-enter the tube matrix from another angle. And again he heard the angry swirl slow down and stop, as if the Hollows were astonished to find another blockade. Gran and Catalina shared a look of almost-optimism.

Now the Hollows decided to attack. It was as if, after being momentarily put off by the Earth-ball barriers, the Hollows had decided they could just plow right through. Gran heard the wind back up to get a running start. Even through the tunnel wall, Gran could hear the Hollows' fury and determination as the force threw itself against an Earth ball. Gran looked over to Catalina, whose eyes were closed tight, as if she expected the ball to pop and the Hollows to run rampant through the matrix, weakening the earth to drag City Hall underground.

But Gran had an inexplicable confidence in the inflated planets, and sure enough, he heard the distinct sound of the Hollows throwing everything they had against the ball and being bounced back, much like Gran had been when, all those weeks ago, he'd tried to walk through a brick wall.

Chapter EIGHTY-ONE

The Hollows didn't like that at all.

They swirled around the tunnels, trying every angle, and every time were rebuffed.

"They're getting tired," Catalina said. "Hear it?"

Gran could hear it. Their ferocity had dimmed. And then the sound of the Hollows diminished steadily to silence. He pulled his ear from the wall.

"Are they gone?" he asked.

Catalina still had her ear to the wall. After a moment, she pulled away and shrugged. Gran was too nervous to smile, but he saw the start of a grin tugging at Catalina's mouth, and he felt his face mirroring hers.

"I think you might have done something here, Gran," she said. She jerked her chin toward the Earth ball in front of them. "I don't know why I never thought of that. I don't know why *no one* else ever thought of it."

"You think it'll hold them?" Gran asked.

Immediately he regretted asking the question. He would have preferred to simply revel in the feeling that he'd defeated the Hollows, and that he'd thought of this new technique to combat them. Now he'd gone and *asked* for doubt.

"For now at least," Catalina said.

Gran thought he saw a new look on Catalina's face, something like respect. She seemed to finally drop her attitude of superiority, her bossy and dismissive tone. He looked at her carefully, and noticed her face change, steadily, from contentment to horror. Her mouth fell agape.

"What?" he asked.

"Behind you," she whispered.

Chapter EIGHTY-TWO

Gran's neck went cold. He knew the Hollows were behind him. Then again, he hadn't seen them. Or heard them.

With a rising dread, he realized that the Hollows had somehow learned how to sneak up. The Hollows that Gran had experienced before were loud, feral, anything but quiet. But somehow they had either learned to be stealthy, or had always known—but simply hadn't bothered to use this skill. In either case, they were smarter than he'd thought.

"What are they doing?" Gran asked Catalina.

"I don't know," she said. "They seem to be waiting. As if they're angry at you and want to confront you, face to face. Then again, maybe they just want to shake your hand."

"I don't think they want to shake my hand."

"You're probably right. They probably want to maul you. Listen. I know how to get us out of here. But when we do this, it has to be perfect. Ready?"

"I am. But you haven't given me the plan yet."

"I was about to. That's why I said 'Ready?'"

"Oh. I thought you meant—"

"Shush! Here's the plan. I'm going to attach my Lift to the ceiling. When I do, I'll use it to lift myself up and kick open the door. At the same time, I'll grab your hand, and the weight of the door opening should throw us both up and into safety. You got it?"

"Not a chance."

The lights in the tunnel began to flicker.

"On three."

The lights went out and returned, though dimly.

"It won't work."

The howling began.

"It's the only way. One. Two. Three."

252

Chapter EIGHTY-THREE

"I can't believe it," Gran said.

They were aboveground again.

Catalina had done what she said she would do. At the moment the Hollows started for them, she leapt up, stuck her Lift to the ceiling, and pulled her legs up, like she would on monkey bars. She kicked the door open, and in the same fluid motion, she grabbed Gran's hand and the weight of the door thrust them both into the cool air above.

They scrambled and closed the door just as Gran had begun to feel the Hollows' cold gusting and hear their wheezy wailing. Gran and Catalina stood, and Gran saw a mess of signs and placards strewn all over the grass. He realized where they were.

"We're on the City Hall lawn," he said.

Catalina gave him a look. "Where else would we be?" she asked. She looked toward the building. Its lights still burned bright. "Looks like everyone inside is okay. And looks like the votes haven't been tabulated yet."

The ground beneath them continued to twitch and roll. This was the first time Gran had been directly above the Hollows, and he was startled that he could see their movements. Wherever the Hollows went, the earth undulated.

"Don't worry," Catalina said. "They're leaving."

"Can they get out?" Gran asked.

"The Hollows? No," she said. "Think of a shark surviving outside the ocean. Not possible."

"What happens to them now?"

"Usually they go away. They amass power and speed and rip through the underground in a fury. But when they're thwarted, they disperse. They're like a defeated army going back to regroup, to regain their strength."

Catalina sat back, her hands on the ground behind her. She looked relaxed in a way Gran had never seen before.

"I think they're whupped for tonight," she said.

"They won't come back?"

"Not today."

"So does that mean I'm a Lifter now?" Gran asked.

"What? No. No. You helped out. You did a good job. You really did. But Lifters have to go through a long process of training and assessment. And it all starts with an elaborate process where you have to make a Lift, and then there are weeks of training just on the lifting . . ."

"But I already have a Lift," Gran said.

"Don't start this again. There's no way you already have a Lift. They have to be made a certain way. By hand."

"Mine is. I'm sure of it."

"Let me see it."

Catalina grabbed it, seeming to be weighing it in her hand. She tossed it to her other hand. Her face implied that she was impressed by it. "That's not a Lift," she said.

"It already worked for me," Gran said.

"Then make it work again," she said.

"I will."

"Then do it. Or don't. I know you're easily embarrassed."

"I don't care," Gran said, feeling a new feeling. Was it confidence? "I'm not about to be embarrassed."

Gran bent down and stuck his handle into the earth. For a moment, his confidence wavered. He had the distinct feeling it wasn't going to work.

But then it did work. A door emerged.

Chapter **EIGHTY-FOUR**

"How'd you do that?" Catalina asked.

Gran had no idea. He'd just found the Lift in his attic and tried it. Then again, it was his great-great-grandfather's work, and that had to mean something. He was trying to think of how to explain it when the doors of City Hall burst open.

"We won!" a woman's voice roared. It was Phyllis Feeley. She was followed by hundreds more, maybe even everyone in town. Most of the faces leaving the building were happy, some were not. The face of Dr. Woolford emerged in the doorway.

"I'll tell you all one thing," he roared to the dispersing crowd. "When a moose attacks, don't come to me for medical help!"

There were laughs from all corners of the City Hall lawn.

"Oh c'mon, Walter," Phyllis Feeley said. "Let me treat you to an ice cream sandwich."

And Gran saw something remarkable: Dr. Woolford agreed. The idea of an ice cream sandwich seemed to soften him, and he smiled and walked toward Phyllis Feeley, and when he was within reach, he extended his hand and Phyllis Feeley took it. They walked together down the street, heading for ice cream sandwiches.

"So I guess we get some money for parks and schools," Catalina said. "That's good news."

Gran watched the door, thinking his mother and Maisie would emerge any minute. He wanted to congratulate his mother, and even thought she would be in the same kind of celebratory mood he was; he thought maybe they'd all go for ice cream sandwiches too. But she and Maisie didn't emerge.

"What are you looking for?" Catalina asked.

"My mom and sister."

A phone rang. The sound was familiar; Gran was sure it was the ring of one of the old-fashioned wall phones that connected to the Regional Manager. Catalina dropped down into the tunnel and answered it. Gran ducked his head into the tunnel to hear her side of the conversation.

"Yes? I know. Okay. Really? I don't know if that's right. Sorry. I know I'm not the Regional Manager. You are. Fine. Sorry. Yes. Sorry. I know. I will. Thank you."

Catalina hung up, and Gran jumped into the tunnel.

"I don't think this is fair," she said.

"What isn't fair?" Gran said.

"It took a lot longer for me," she said.

"What did?"

"To become a Lifter."

"So I'm a Lifter?" Gran asked.

"No. But the Regional Manager says that you're an exception. He knows you found or made your own Lift, and made it work. And apparently that gives you the right to attend the Hemispheric Conference."

Gran swelled with something like pride.

"It's not fair. I waited two years before my first conference." Catalina was doing something Gran never thought possible of her: she was pouting.

"When is it?" he asked.

This practical question, and its practical answer, seemed to snap Catalina out of her funk. "It's in about an hour," she said. "We better get going. I'll explain on the way down."

Chapter **EIGHTY-FIVE**

"**D**own?" Gran asked.

Catalina led him through some tunnels he'd seen before, and some he hadn't. They ran for what seemed like miles as the tunnels wound up and down and left and right. And finally Catalina turned to him.

"You trust me, yes?"

"Sure," Gran said, unsure. He did trust Catalina, but when someone asks if you trust them, it usually means they're about to do something that will make you reassess that trust.

"I'm going to open this door," she said, putting her Lift into what seemed like a vertical rock wall. "And when I do, I'm going to drop, and I'll drop for a long time. You'll do the same thing right after me. Or you can do it first. You want to go first?"

Gran didn't know where they were going, so he said no, he didn't want to go first.

"Fine," Catalina continued, "when I drop, and when you drop, it'll seem like you're dropping for about four or five miles."

"But what?" Gran said, interrupting.

"I didn't say *but*," Catalina said.

"It seemed like you were saying it would seem like you're dropping for about four or five miles, but . . ."

"I never said *but*," Catalina corrected. "It seems like you're dropping for four or five miles because that's how far you're dropping."

"Wait. We're dropping four or five miles? To where?"

"Something like that. It's really hard to tell. It hasn't been measured. It's not like you can take a tape measure to the walls of the chute."

"It's a chute?"

"That's the closest thing I can compare it to. It's a tube and it goes down. So it's a chute. We can talk on the way. Ready?"

Chapter **EIGHTY-SIX**

Bravery has its limits. Bravery sometimes needs a rest.

Shortly after Gran saved City Hall through his courage and ingenuity, Catalina had just suggested that he drop through the Earth four or five miles, to attend something called the Hemispheric Conference, which Gran knew nothing about. (Catalina had promised to explain it on the way, but was that really okay? That's like explaining skydiving while you're falling from an airplane.)

Standing there, in front of a seemingly bottomless hole, Gran had the thought that maybe he had done enough brave things for that day.

He pictured his home, and his mother and Maisie, and his father far away, and he wanted to be with them. He wanted to take a bath and sit on the couch in dry clothes, watching TV as Maisie pretended to be a cat. He decided he wanted that. To be home and safe and dry and warm. He did not want to leap into a miles-long lightless chute.

"Ready?" Catalina said again.

"I think I should go home," Gran said.

"What? You can't go home. After all that? You followed me around for weeks. You kept saying you wanted to help. *Please, please,* on and on. Now the Regional Manager gives you this opportunity, and all you have to do is jump into the center of the Earth for a while, and you're going to back out?"

"Exactly," Gran said. "I don't even really know what I was thinking. I don't know what it is to be a Lifter anyway. You were right. I'm not qualified."

Catalina reached out for Gran's hand, and he had the momentary fear that she planned to fling him into the chute. Of all the people he'd known in his life, Catalina Catalan, who had punched him and kicked him, seemed the most likely to fling him into a five-mile vertical tunnel leading into the inner mantle of the Earth.

But when she grabbed his hand with her rough hands, she simply turned his wrist to look at his watch.

"We have one minute. If we're going to make it in time, we have to leave in sixty seconds."

"That makes it easy. I don't want to go. There. We only spent two seconds. You have fifty-eight seconds left."

Catalina did something unexpected. Gran thought she would either hit him, or say something mean to him, or just jump into the hole herself. But instead she leaned back against the wall of the tunnel, and she sighed.

"When I first met you," she said, "I saw your watch. It's kind of a fancy watch, so I assumed a lot. I assumed you were rich. And that you were the kind of kid who wears a watch, which is itself unusual. To have a fancy watch and be willing to wear it, I figured you were some rich airhead who I'd want to punch in the gut."

"You *did* punch me in the gut," Gran noted.

"But that wasn't because of your *watch*," Catalina clarified. "Anyway, because of the watch, I figured you weren't serious about anything, and that there was no possibility that you'd ever been sad. So when you said you wanted to be a Lifter, I said no way. Because to be a Lifter, you have to be serious, and you have to be brave, and just as importantly, you have to know sadness."

"Why?" Gran said. He was intrigued.

"Because sadness is duty," Catalina said. "Do you understand?"

"No. How is sadness duty?"

"Because if you know sadness, you understand sadness in others. And if you can understand sadness in others, you're obligated to help."

She saw Gran's blank look. Gran had certainly known sadness, because he saw it every night in the eyes of his mother, and he saw it on the faces of many of the people of Carousel. But his concept of sadness was more a solitary thing. It seemed to him a thing experienced alone, a thing that rightly or wrongly made you look inward. The notion that Catalina had just explained, though, was utterly opposed to that kind of self-centeredness.

"If you know sadness, you want to help lessen it," she explained. "Improve things. Brighten the days. Lift people up. You know?"

Gran thought he understood. Almost.

"Yes," he said.

"So we prop up the tunnels the Hollows make. Get it?"

"I get it."

"Because if we strengthen what's underneath, we might allow for happiness above."

Gran didn't completely understand.

Catalina looked exasperated. "If we strengthen what's underneath, we might allow for happiness above. No? ¿No comprende?"

Gran thought he understood. But he wasn't sure he understood. It was all very confusing. But while Catalina was explaining the Lifters' work, something had happened to Gran. He had begun to feel like he wanted to jump with her. That he didn't need to be home and warm on the couch. That he wanted to see what was in the chute. He wanted to see what was next.

"Okay," Gran said. "I'll go."

"You will?" Catalina said, seeming more surprised than Gran expected. "Wow, I'm good. I mean, I knew I was good, but I didn't expect that little speech to convince you. I'm impressed with myself."

Catalina's crooked smile overtook her face.

"But we should go. Let me see your watch again," she said, and grabbed his wrist.

But instead of looking at the time, she jumped into the void, and pulled Gran with her.

Chapter EIGHTY-SEVEN

Falling toward the center of the Earth is something few people have done. Statistically, the number of people who have done this would have to be somewhere between 2 and 5 percent. Maybe lower.

For a while it feels just like diving from a high board at the pool: there is the same weightlessness and wind in one's hair. But then it does not end.

"It'll end eventually," Catalina said, her voice rushing up. That is, at the moment she spoke, Gran had already fallen a hundred feet below her words. They were distant, faint, shooting far above as he descended. Stranger still, Gran could not see Catalina. He couldn't see anything. He could feel nothing but the wind under his arms, the wind that shot up through his shirt. It was sending his shirt into his face, which was profoundly uncomfortable.

"I usually tuck in my shirt," Catalina noted.

Gran thought it impossible to tuck in his shirt while falling through the inner mantle of the Earth, but when he tried, he found that just about anything he normally could do, he could do while descending.

So he pulled the shirt off his face and tucked it into his khakis, and immediately felt more comfortable. There was no more wind shooting up through his collar, but there was the occasional feel-ing that he might hit one of the tunnel walls, or an out-cropping. He pictured a pebble thrown down a well—if it even skimmed the wall of the well, it would careen wildly off course.

"Keep your arms and legs in if you can," Catalina said.

Eventually, any steady thing can become routine. People fly in airplanes every hour of every day, and we forget that they are metal tubes shooting through space near the speed of sound. It is not a routine thing, to fly through the air in a metal tube, watching TV or sleeping while we do this, but it becomes routine.

And so it was with Gran falling through the Earth. He was afraid to do it, and then startled by the feeling of blackness and speed and the unknown below him. Then, after a few minutes, he wondered when it would be over.

"Almost over," Catalina said.

And moments later, Gran felt himself slow. The air below him seemed to become more dense, or more resistant.

"There's an updraft here," Catalina explained. "It slows you down, then eventually it'll stop us altogether."

The air became thicker, and Gran's progress slowed to the point where he could reach out to the shiny-smooth wall of the chute and feel their speed—which was about the speed of a Ferris wheel.

"Get ready for light," Catalina said. "It'll take a second for your eyes to adjust."

Gran looked down, and saw a pinpoint of butter-colored light.

"That's where we get off," Catalina said. Gran looked to her, and could see her face, ever so faintly, in the growing illumination from below.

"How do we stop?" he asked.

"We'll stop," she said.

Chapter EIGHTY-EIGHT

But first they slowed. The resistance beneath them grew stronger until they were floating above it, perfectly still. Gran was loving it, hovering and somersaulting in midair, but soon he noticed that Catalina was already standing in the tunnel next to him, tapping her foot impatiently.

"We have to go," she said, and yanked him from the air current. He collapsed in the tunnel like a bag of oranges.

"Thank you," Gran said.

He could hear voices, hundreds of them, down the tunnel.

"Hurry," Catalina said, and pulled him along.

The tunnel was sturdier, more permanent, than the ones closer to the surface, and there were tiles underfoot—a patchwork of

round tiles of various colors. Above, there was a string of lights mounted on the rounded ceiling.

As they hurried down the hall, the voices grew louder and Gran detected an echo, as if whatever room or cavern the voices were in was enormous.

Gran followed Catalina around two tight turns, one left and one right, and then stopped. The tunnel had opened like a river to the sea. The room before them was vast. It sloped gently downward, like a theater, until it leveled out at what appeared to be the stage. There were easily a thousand people in the room, almost all of them kids like Gran and Catalina, every one of them about the same

height they were. There was an
air of excitement and welcome,
a cross between family reunion
and rock concert.

"Who are these people?"
Gran asked.

"Don't play dumb,"
Catalina said.

Gran knew they were Lifters. Now he began to notice their Lifts in their hands and back pockets. A few wore them around their necks. Some were silver and ornate, as Catalina's was. Others were simple and made of wood.

"I didn't know there were so many," he said.

"One for every town, Gran. At least," Catalina said. "How could everything hold up without us?"

Because most of the Lifters were dressed up—or at least dressed with clean clothes—Gran wished he weren't wearing the same khakis, drenched and dried with urine and milk and water, that he'd been wearing for a full day now.

"Don't worry about your pants," Catalina said. Gran couldn't decide how he felt about Catalina's ever-increasing ability to read his mind. Was it good to be known so well? He decided it was good. With Catalina it was good.

As they moved through the crowd, Gran heard other languages, Spanish and Portuguese among them, but the rest he couldn't name. There were too many to count.

"We need to get closer," Catalina said. "You should get a good look at the new Hemispheric Commissioner. They're chosen from the Regional Manager ranks, and they rotate every year. This one's brand-new, just appointed. This is his first conference."

Finally Gran and Catalina were at the front of the crowd, pressed against the stage. Gran looked upward to see a vaulting dome that reminded him of his old church by the sea. It was carved from the stone, with a constellation of rough gemstones embedded. In the torchlight they sparkled red and gold and emerald green.

"I can't believe I'm here," Gran said.

"Well, you are," Catalina replied.

Then Gran felt very grateful to Catalina. At school, when he was new and knew nothing, she had been the only one to care about him, to listen to him. Even that first day, when he had tried to walk through a wall, she had lifted him up. That small act of noticing him when no one else did, that brief act of caring—just one person seeing another's struggle and bringing them to their feet again—it was the difference between a cold world of being forever apart, and a world where one could feel bound to another, obligated to kindness. He wanted to tell her all of this, but instead he just quietly said, "Thank you."

Catalina smiled. "I was wondering when you were going to say that. You're welcome."

Then her attention was turned to the stage. A petite woman was walking from the wings to the microphone just a few feet away from where Gran and Catalina stood. A roar of applause started in the back of the room and swept forward.

"This is the outgoing Hemispheric Commissioner," Catalina whispered.

"What's her name?" Gran asked.

"That's it. Hemispheric Commissioner. With the Regional Managers and Commissioners, that's all we know. No first names, no real names. When they serve in those capacities, they're anonymous."

She was now just in front of Gran and Catalina. She looked about the age of Gran's mother, though she was smaller than most adult women he'd encountered. In fact, she looked no taller than Gran and Catalina. She was wearing what Gran thought was a tuxedo, though he wasn't sure if he'd ever seen a tuxedo on a woman before. She tapped the microphone and smiled.

"Attention, Lifters," she said. Her eyes crinkled when she said that, and Gran knew he liked her. Those who smile with their eyes are surely the most likable of people.

"Welcome to the Hemispheric Conference!" she said.

The crowd roared again. Gran turned around to see that a thousand kids were holding up their Lifts. Catalina nudged him, and he saw that she was holding hers overhead too. He fumbled in his pocket and brought out his own Lift.

"Go on," Catalina said.

Gran raised his arm. At first he was embarrassed. He never liked to make dramatic

movements like this, especially with so many people around. Then, just when he was getting comfortable with this gesture of belonging and pride, another feeling seized him—the feeling that he might not be worthy.

As if reading his mind, Catalina leaned into him. "It's okay. You belong here," she said.

Finally Gran allowed himself to feel at one with everyone around him and everything they stood for. He allowed himself to feel awake and giddy and good.

Chapter EIGHTY-NINE

"All right," the Hemispheric Commissioner said after a time. "Lower your Lifts, please."

The Lifters settled down, and the look on the Hemispheric Commissioner's face grew somber.

"As most of you know, I was once like you. Lifters start young, and most of us grow too big to stay in the work. A Lifter, of course, should be nimble and strong and brave and clever, sure, but we also have to be small."

The audience chuckled in appreciation of this essential fact.

"I was lucky enough to remain small into adulthood, which provided me the good fortune to remain a Lifter all my life. And I was lucky enough to rise to the rank of Regional Manager, and finally Hemispheric Commissioner. It has been the honor of my life to serve in this capacity. But every Commissioner's tenure must come to an end, and I now have the pleasure of introducing my successor."

A buzz overtook the crowd.

"He is, like me, a lifetime Lifter, and over the past few weeks, as we've exchanged information and expertise, he has become my friend. I can't possibly express how much faith I have in his ability to lead us through what are undoubtedly troubling times. Without further ado, I hereby introduce, and bestow upon this Lifter the mantle of, Hemispheric Commissioner."

The outgoing Hemispheric Commissioner bowed and walked toward a wing of the stage. The audience applauded wildly as her successor took the floor.

It was the Duke.

Chapter **NINETY**

There is something unusual that happens to humans when they see someone—for example, their dentist or local librarian—in an entirely different or unexpected context—for example, at a wedding and doing the limbo. Their brains jam. Just as gears can jam, causing an engine to sputter and stall, your brain can get so crossed up that it temporarily stops functioning.

This is what happened to Gran.

He had traveled miles into the inner mantle of the Earth. He was with Catalina Catalan, who he knew from his life on the surface, but he did not expect to see anyone else from that life. Not his mother or father. Not Maisie. Not Mr. Plain or Ms. Hamid. And certainly not the Duke. The Duke's domain was the storage room at Carousel Middle School. How could he have gotten here?

"That's the Duke," Gran said to Catalina.

"Who's the Duke?" she asked.

"That guy walking onto the stage. He's the Duke. He works at our **school**."

Catalina looked befuddled. "The guy in the basement? Can't be," she said. "You're nuts." Then Catalina turned her attention to the man at the microphone, who Gran was certain was the Duke, but who Catalina saw only as the incoming Hemispheric Commissioner, meaning he was in charge of all Lifters in North and South America.

"Greetings, fellow Lifters," the man said, and now Gran was sure he was the Duke. He had the Duke's same faint accent, his same excited tone of voice.

Gran looked at Catalina. Her face was frozen, her mouth hanging open.

"As most of you know," the Duke continued, "we're in the middle of a period of unprecedented Hollows activity. I know it from my own territory. There, things have been tough. Much Hollows activity—more than I've seen in my lifetime. Luckily, we have some extremely hardworking and innovative Lifters covering my municipality . . ." And here the Duke looked down at Gran and Catalina and winked.

Gran was shocked. Catalina almost fainted.

"But we must be on the highest alert," the Duke continued. "Things are falling down, and we must be there to hold them up."

The crowd cheered. Gran, afraid of offending the Duke, who was now his boss and the leader of a thousand Lifters, cheered, too. Catalina, meanwhile, remained frozen.

"He was the Regional Manager all along," she said, as if in a trance. "I know the voice. But I never met him. We don't meet the RMs."

As the Duke continued, both Gran and Catalina drifted off mentally as they tried to put the facts together. It was complicated but not impossible, Gran thought. Of course the Duke might have been a Lifter—his size made him perfect for the role. And of course Catalina wouldn't have known him—she only knew him through his phone calls. Gran had met him another way, not knowing he was the RM; indeed, Gran had met the Duke before he had any inkling about the Lifters one way or another. But then, when the Duke had given him the Earth balls, the Duke must have known why—he knew what Gran was doing. He'd been on the phone with Catalina that day, that night. He'd probably been aware of Gran's work with her all the while!

"Now I get it," Gran said.

Catalina hadn't moved. Gran pulled on her sleeve.

"It's not that hard to believe," he said.

"I can't believe I didn't connect the dots," she said. "I'm usually so smart, but here I was so stupid."

Gran didn't mind hearing Catalina take herself down a notch. It was not an everyday thing for her. She continued staring ahead, her mouth silently moving, still working it all out in her mind.

"We should be listening to the speech," Gran said.

Finally Catalina left her reverie, and they turned their attention back to the Duke, aka the Hemispheric Commissioner. The rest of the crowd was enthralled. Gran was astonished that the eccentric man hidden in the storage closet at school could command the attention—the rapt devotion—of thousands of loyal Lifters.

"The work ahead is difficult and without end," he said. His voice was becoming more commanding with every sentence. "Who among you feels daunted?" he bellowed.

No one raised a hand. No one made a sound.

"The work ahead will tire us and will frustrate us, and victories will be brief and quickly reversed. Who among you is unwilling?"

No one raised a hand. No one made a sound.

"The work we do will be frightening. And dangerous. And dirty. Who among you is afraid?"

No one raised a hand. No one made a sound.

"Good," the Duke said. "Because I believe in you. I believe you can keep the world upright. Or do I have the wrong group of people here? Are we not Lifters?"

"We are Lifters!" the crowd shouted.

"Again," the Duke yelled. "Are we not Lifters?"

"We are Lifters!" they roared.

Chapter **NINETY-ONE**

There was revelry. There were strategy meetings. There were exchanges of ideas. Comparisons of Lifts. There was talk of Gran's innovation with the Earth balls, and how that method might be used to fight the Hollows elsewhere. Most of all, there were stories about battles, from Nova Scotia to Tierra del Fuego, against the Hollows.

"This is the third one of these I've been to," Catalina said. "But this is the biggest by far. A lot of new faces."

The ranks of the Lifters had been growing. This was a popular topic among the thousands of Lifters at the conference. In most regions, they were recruiting new Lifters. And in some places, Lifters were coming out of nowhere. With more activity from the Hollows, more Lifters were needed, and they had to be trained quickly.

"Like you," Catalina said to Gran.

Gran lost track of time. There were parties, there was dancing, and finally everyone was so exhausted they slept where they'd been standing—in the same great hall. They slept overlapping, using legs and stomachs as pillows, and when Gran woke up, he was sure he'd never known such belonging and such purpose.

"Grant," a voice whispered. "Catalina."

Gran looked up to see the Duke standing over them.

"Follow me," the Duke whispered.

Gran and Catalina stood up and followed the Duke out of the hall, stepping over hundreds of sleeping Lifters as they did. The Duke led Gran and Catalina down a dim hallway and into a room that looked almost exactly like the Duke's office in the storage room at Carousel Middle School. There was the same sort of couch, the same sort of coffee table, the same kind of file cabinet, and in it, the same kind of turntable. The Duke set a record spinning and dropped the needle. Cuban music emerged.

"I like to have things a certain way," the Duke said. "You hungry?" he asked, and retrieved a sandwich from another file cabinet. He took a great bite and sat down.

"I can't believe I never realized it was you," Catalina said.

"I'm sorry I couldn't tell you guys much," he said. "But I'm sure you can understand why secrecy is important to this whole operation."

There were a hundred questions Gran and Catalina wanted to ask, but Gran could only think of one.

"A few days ago, Catalina said something about erasing my memory. Can you guys actually do that?"

"Oh, sorry about that," the Duke said. "I was just spitballing. I don't know how to do that. But I saw it in a movie once."

Gran felt great relief, and though he had ninety-nine more questions, it was time for the Duke to ask one of his own.

"Grant, can I see your Lift?"

Gran handed him the brass C.

The Duke laughed with delight. "I had a feeling. You know what this is, don't you?"

"A Lift," Gran said.

"Yes, but do you know what it was originally?"

Gran shrugged. "My great-great-grandfather made it."

"Was he a blacksmith?" the Duke asked.

"I think so," Gran said.

"So you understand?" the Duke asked.

Gran didn't understand.

"This is a horseshoe!" the Duke said. "But not a regular horseshoe. This was a special one. It wasn't made for a real horse, but a carousel horse. It's no wonder it worked as a Lift. Lifts should have personal meaning to the user. They should have history, because history is power. Do you understand?"

Now Gran understood.

"My Lift is just a handle I found near the old factory," Catalina said. She seemed dejected, as if her Lift's history couldn't possibly match that of Gran's.

"Catalina!" the Duke roared, a big open smile lighting up his face. "I can't believe you didn't know what you were holding! You really don't know?"

"I really don't know," she said flatly.

"That isn't just some handle. That's the handle that opened the front door of the factory! The door a thousand workers passed through—ten thousand visitors. They had tours there every weekend, and kids and dignitaries and everyone in between came through! Can you imagine? It was so beautiful. So many of us who worked there stayed on Saturdays just to see it. To show the people how we did what we did. It was a joyous day."

Catalina's face softened. She almost smiled.

"And that beautiful piece of metal in your hand opened the door, every day for decades. Everyone who ever set foot in the factory touched that handle first. It was the way into the best thing that ever happened to this town."

Finally Catalina's mouth turned upward. Her teeth emerged. She grinned like she'd never grinned before.

Chapter **NINETY-TWO**

"Have you had a good time down here?" the Duke asked them both.

Gran said he had.

"I remember my first HC," the Duke said. "Back then it was only a few hundred of us. But it was important to see each other. There's great strength that comes from knowing you're not alone in the fight." He turned to Catalina. "Don't you agree?"

Catalina nodded solemnly.

The Duke continued. "And there's something about knowing that the battles continue all over the world. Not just in this hemisphere, by the way. Sometime soon you'll attend the World Gathering, and there you'll see everyone—a global force never before assembled in the history of the world. I think you'll like that."

All Gran could say was "Yes."

"But listen, you two. I want you to remember something very crucial to all this. Though you're here among Lifters from everywhere—from Winnipeg and Wyoming and Oaxaca and Peru—your work will always be where you live. In Carousel. Do you understand that?"

"I do," Catalina said.

Gran felt something drop into his shoe. It seemed like his stomach. He hadn't thought of home in days.

"Will you come back?" Catalina asked the Duke.

"Of course," the Duke said. "My home's still in Carousel. I'll follow you in a few days. You keep things safe in the meantime, okay?"

Gran and Catalina said they would. But Gran's mind was preoccupied.

"Speaking of home," the Duke said, as if reading his thoughts, "when was the last time you checked in with your parents? Do they know where you are?"

Chapter NINETY-THREE

"Why did you get so weird all of a sudden in there?" Catalina asked.

They had left the Duke's office and were standing outside his door.

"How do I get back to Carousel?" Gran asked.

"You have to take the stairs," Catalina said. "There's going to be an elevator, but it's not ready yet. Are you telling me your parents have no idea where you are?"

"No. Do yours?"

"My mom thinks I'm staying at a friend's house. She had to work double shifts, so I said I'd be at Katie Cabinet's house."

"Who's Katie Cabinet?" Gran asked. He was sure there was no such person at their school.

"I made her up," Catalina said. "My mom has no idea who goes to our school."

Normally Gran would have laughed, but his mind was darting around his skull like a squirrel caught in a sack. "How long have we been gone?" he asked. "And did you say I had to take the stairs? Five miles of stairs?"

"They're working on a better system, but it's not like you can just install an elevator to the inner mantle of the Earth overnight."

"Where are they?"

"The stairs?"

"No, the Pope. Yes, the stairs."

Catalina led him through a series of hallways until they met the entrance to a stairway that looked in every way like the kind of stairs you'd use to get to or from an underground parking garage.

"You staying?" he asked Catalina.

"For another day, yes," she said. "There's still a lot I have to learn."

Gran poked his head into the stairwell. "You've done this before. How long will it take?"

Chapter **NINETY-FOUR**

It took him a while. Most of the day. Actually, all of the day. The trip was exhausting and lonely, and all the while, Gran thought of his mother, how worried she would be. He'd been gone more than a day. She would have called his father. They would have called the police.

Gran tried to take his mind off all that. He counted the steps, and after fifteen thousand he gave up. By the time he reached the door where he and Catalina had begun their descent, he was sure he'd climbed at least thirty thousand, but wouldn't have been surprised if it was twice that.

At the door, though, he sensed the vastness of the world aboveground, and he felt a surge of new strength. He inserted his Lift into the solid granite wall, turned, and pulled. The night sky greeted him; the fresh air filled his weary lungs. He felt proud, and he smiled. He felt the pride and wore the smile of someone who has done a lot in one day—there is no greater pride a human can feel than when you've filled a few days with the sights and deeds of a year. It's like beating time. It's like slowing the turning of the globe.

Gran's pleasure, though, was short-lived.

He had to go home. And he knew there would be trouble at home. But he had to face it, and he had to hurry.

He ran toward his house, and as he did, he imagined what his mother would say to him, and what he could possibly say to appease her. Could he say he had been caught in a bear trap? That he'd been kidnapped by rogue scientists forcing him to test jetpack technology?

Chapter **NINETY-FIVE**

When he saw his house in the distance, he paused.

All excuses involving bear traps and rogue scientists fell away. He knew he had to tell his mother the truth—or some version of the truth that she'd believe. He knew he couldn't tell her about the Lifters, and about plunging to the center of the Earth. That would probably worry her, he thought.

He would tell her that he was with a friend, and they were helping the town. And all of a sudden it all came together for him. He *did* have a plan to help the town.

I'm sorry, he would say.

It was wrong to be gone without telling you.

But it will all be better soon. So much better.

Let me tell you my idea . . .

His plan in place, he strode to the house on confident feet. Then, when he was just across the street, he stopped.

He forgot to breathe.

Chapter **NINETY-SIX**

Something was moving. Everything was moving. The mailbox jerked as if struck by an invisible bat. Then the hedge next to it shook. Then the tree next to the hedge vibrated. Gran looked at the ground and saw the grass shivering. The path of all the activity was moving steadily around the house in concentric circles and getting closer.

It was the Hollows.

He didn't know what to do. Could he use his Lift to get underearth and distract them? He wished Catalina were with him.

Why would they be here? Gran wondered.

Then the circle became a straight line. The Hollows cut inward and struck the corner of the house. The porch buckled.

A shriek came from inside. His mother. Then another: Maisie. The Hollows must have cut through the corner post of the porch. Gran's house was under attack.

Gran ran across the street, leapt over the mounds created by the Hollows, and flew up the steps and into the house.

"Mom?" he yelled.

"Gran?" she said. "In here."

He found them in the kitchen, hiding in the broom closet. His mother's wheelchair had been abandoned and she was curled up beside the vacuum cleaner, with Maisie under her folded legs. He'd never seen the two of them look so small and so scared.

The house shook. Glasses poured out of the cabinets and shattered on the floor.

"Where have you been?" she asked over the noise. "What's happening here? Is it another sinkhole?"

Gran had never heard his mother so afraid, so uncertain.

"Get under here with us!" she insisted.

Gran stood above them. He was a Lifter now, and had just been to the inner mantle of the Earth. He couldn't cower in a closet. "There's no room for me," he said calmly. "Mom, I think we need to leave."

"No," she hissed. "Too dangerous. Get in here!" Now her voice was fierce. It reminded him that he was his mother's son. He could not defy her.

He crawled into the closet, and they were soon stuffed together like three hot dogs in a jewelry box.

She held him against her chest and kissed the crown of his head.

"Where were you?" she asked, her voice kinder now.

"Long story," he said. "But I'm fine."

"I was so worried," she said. "The police were here. And your father's almost home. He's been driving for eight hours. We've been talking all the while. I was crying, and finally he was crying, and we both thought something terrible had happened to you."

"Mama was so sad," Maisie said. "That's when the earthquake happened."

From below, they heard a sudden rumble. It grew louder, as if the Hollows were directly beneath them, trying to plow up from below and take Gran's family under.

"It's not an earthquake," Gran said. "You have to trust me. We need to get out of this closet."

"Why?" his mother asked.

"I can't explain," he said.

"Then we're not leaving," she said.

The rumble grew louder, closer and more concentrated, as if there were only a few feet separating the floor they were sitting on from the swirling Hollows below.

Chapter **NINETY-SEVEN**

They stayed in the closet, but Gran knew they needed to leave.

He knew he couldn't tell his mother and Maisie what was really happening. His mother wouldn't believe it and Maisie would be terrified.

But he knew the Hollows were drawn by despair, and his house was full of it.

"Hey, Maisie," he said, and he tried to tickle her.

She slapped his hand and pretended he'd hurt her. The rumbling from the Hollows grew louder, closer.

The house was shaking wildly now. Plates crashed on the kitchen floor. Above, there was a thump and the sound of shattering glass.

"Picture frame," Maisie said. "I'm scared!"

Gran was desperate. "Smile, Mom," he said. "Got to stay positive!"

"What are you talking about? How can we stay positive?" There were tears in her eyes.

The front door crashed open, wailing on its hinges, and a wind gusted in. Gran had a horrible vision that the Hollows had found a way to survive aboveground and had entered the house. He pulled the closet door shut, threw himself over his mother and Maisie, and waited for the worst.

A thumping came from the porch. Now Gran was sure the Hollows were coming for them.

Thump. Thump.

The thumping seemed to be determined but confused.

"Where is everyone?" a voice yelled. It was a voice Gran hadn't heard in a month: Gran's father.

The thumping had been his heavy boots.

"We're in here!" his mother said.

The broom closet door swung open and there he was.

He was home.

He looked both tired and alarmed. His eyes were ringed with sleeplessness, but there was worry there, and relief, and a sadness that spoke of his regret that he was away while his family was in danger.

"You all right?" he asked. He fell to his knees and took them all into his arms. They huddled there in the closet, with Maisie squatting in the middle, smiling to see her father back, to have her mother and father and brother encircle her. They stayed like that for only a few minutes, but it seemed far longer. Gran could smell the stale sweat of his father, who had been cooped up in the car so long, racing home. Tears left his father's eyes, then his mother's. Soon the three of them were crying—everyone but Maisie, who wasn't sure exactly what was happening. "The house was shaking," she said to her father.

And when she said that, it dawned on Gran that the shaking had ended. The house was no longer under attack. He went to the front of the house, where he looked out the window. By the mailbox he could see the slightest vibration in the grass. It was as if the Hollows were waiting out there, assessing Gran's family for signs of vulnerability.

"What are you looking for, Granite?" his father asked.

Gran felt something tighten around his hand, and he realized it was his father's big mitt of a hand. They hadn't held hands in years, and Gran had forgotten how it felt. His father's fingers were large and his palm was callused; his skin felt like the fabric on their couch. But his father's hand was warm, too, and having his own hand held like that gave Gran a feeling of indescribable comfort and strength.

Gran turned to find his mother wheeling through the front door, with Maisie sitting on her lap.

"Is it over?" his mother asked.

"Is what over?" his father asked. He pointed to the crooked porch, which was listing heavily to the right. "Someone please tell me what happened."

Chapter NINETY-EIGHT

G ran knew he had to tell his family the whole story. With the Hollows gone, they settled into the family room and Gran began from the beginning.

He told his family about meeting Catalina. About following her through the hills and valleys. About her disappearing into the Earth. About finding his own Lift and following her into the tunnels. About being attacked by the Hollows. About the implosion of the home of Therése and Theresa. About helping Catalina prop up the tunnels with hockey sticks and car fenders. About meeting the Duke. About the sinkhole in the school. About saving City Hall. About being invited to the Hemispheric Conference, which required falling into the inner mantle of the Earth. About the Duke turning out to be the Hemispheric Commissioner. And about returning from the conference to find his own house under attack. About how Gran's great-great-grandfather was a blacksmith who made horseshoes not for real horses but for carousel animals.

Once he explained it all, Gran looked at his parents, and at Maisie, and he realized that his story sounded nuts. He was pretty sure they didn't believe anything he'd just said.

And he was correct.

"That's some story, Granite," his father said. "I always knew you were creative, but that's a doozy. Well done."

His father didn't believe it. Neither did his mom or Maisie. And it was just as well. If he was to continue to be a Lifter, his parents couldn't know. They wouldn't let him run through the tunnels, risking his own life to save the town above.

But he needed to do exactly that.

Chapter **NINETY-NINE**

In the morning, Gran woke to the sounds of activity downstairs. He heard his mother's exclamations. Something exciting was happening. Something very good.

Gran got dressed, noting through the window that the morning was bright and looked warm for late October. It was Sunday, he remembered—the most welcome of days. He needed a rest.

He found his mother in the kitchen, sitting on a new wheelchair. It was far more modern and elaborate than her old one. "Dad got it used and fixed it," Maisie said.

"Easier to get up and down the hills with this one," he said.

"Look," Gran's mother said, grinning, and she moved a lever

on the armrest, causing the chair to lurch forward. "It's automatic, see?" she said. Just then, Maisie's face emerged from behind Gran's mother. Seeing the two of them together, Gran's mother and Maisie, Gran thought for a moment how young they both looked. For a moment they looked like twins.

Chapter **ONE HUNDRED**

They had work to do (to repair the porch), and they had
cleaning to do (to collect the broken dishes scattered all over
the kitchen), but it was nothing. Work like that, with your family
on a sunny Sunday—it's nothing.

Gran's mom put on the radio, and while they worked and
cleaned, she shimmied in her new chair, and Maisie jumped on the
couch, and was told to stop jumping on the couch, and she did, and
then she threw up.

But it was nothing.

They cleaned up Maisie's mess together, and after the house
was tidy and Gran's father had propped up the porch with two-by-
fours—more permanent repairs would follow—they went for a

walk around the neighborhood, to test out the new motorized wheelchair.

Maisie rode on their mother's lap, her face aglow. As they walked, she turned around, again and again, to make sure their father was still with them.

They walked all over.

They walked past the old Catalan Carousel factory, and Gran told Maisie and his parents what he knew about it. They walked past the grocery store and the flea market, and then they passed City Hall, which looked pristine, totally undisturbed.

Then he remembered his idea.

Chapter **ONE HUNDRED AND ONE**

It had been at the forefront of Gran's mind until the Hollows had circled, when his father's return had taken precedence in Gran's world. Now, though, seeing City Hall again brought it all back.

He had devised a plan.

Now was the time to set the plan in motion.

After the family walk, when they were all home again and sitting in the backyard, enjoying the last hour of daylight through the dappling trees, Gran asked his mother if he could run a quick errand.

"Sure," she said.

"And I'll need your old wheelchair," he said.

Normally she might be skeptical, and would probably say no, but she was so bursting with the day's warmth, and having her family together and around her, that she only said, "Don't scuff it up again, please. And be back by dinner."

Gran took his Lift, and a shovel—he didn't bother telling anyone he was borrowing it, because who would care about a borrowed shovel?—and he raced the chair down the hill and over to City Hall. There, when no one was looking, he created a door where there had been no door, and pushed the chair in, and then followed.

"What are you doing here?" Catalina asked. Or rather, Catalina's voice asked. Gran couldn't see her at first.

"Where are you?" he asked.

"Over here," she said. "Give me a hand."

He wound his way through the tunnel matrix, most of its paths still jammed by Gran's Earth-ball blockade, until he found her.

She was doing exactly what he'd planned to do himself.

Chapter **ONE HUNDRED AND TWO**

S he was digging out the carousel horse they'd seen under City
Hall. The horse's face was exposed, but the rest of its body was
lodged in the tunnel wall.

"Great minds," she said.

"What?" Gran said.

"Great minds think alike. You know that expression?"

Gran had not heard the expression, but chose not to reveal this
to Catalina. As always when she was engaged in a task, she got a
little bossy.

"You need help?" he asked.

"I just said I did," she said. "Careful, though. There's already
enough damage. Don't be a klutz."

That was enough. Gran was a Lifter now, too, and the idea of digging out the horse, and bringing it to the Duke, had been his idea too. He didn't have to be Catalina's assistant.

"I'll help if you stop acting like my boss, okay?" he said. "I brought my mom's chair so we could carry it to the Duke. Bet you didn't think of that."

Catalina paused, looked Gran square in the face, and laughed. "Fine. Sorry. You're right. Let's get this sucker out and to the Duke. I can't wait to see his face."

Chapter ONE HUNDRED AND THREE

With the two of them working steadily, the job only took an hour. When they were done, the horse lay on the tunnel floor looking like it had run a mile through the mud. It was brown and black with dirt, and there were chunks missing from its mane and chest.

"And it lost a leg," Catalina noted.

Gran hadn't seen that until she pointed it out. But the horse was indeed lacking a rear hind leg, at least below the hock. In all, there was more damage than Gran had expected, but it didn't seem to be more than the Duke could handle.

They loaded the horse—which was far heavier than either of them had thought possible—onto the wheelchair and pushed it out of the tunnel.

"You sure he's back?" Gran asked.

"I know he is," Catalina said. "We took the elevator up together."

Gran was dumbfounded. "What elevator? I climbed thirty thousand steps."

"I know. Sorry about that. They finished the elevator the day after you left."

Chapter ONE HUNDRED AND FOUR

"**D**uke?" Gran said.

The door had been open, and, wanting to surprise the Duke, Gran and Catalina had wheeled in the chair bearing the horse.

When the Duke emerged from the rear of the room, his face cycled through a series of expressions before he managed to speak.

First, he seemed alarmed that a large new object was in his storage space. Gran knew the Duke always flinched when someone brought something new in and expected him to find room for it.

Then there was the slow process of discerning just what this new object was.

Next, he recognized it as a horse.

Then, surprise again overtook his expression, as he seemed to wonder why a wooden carousel horse would be in his domain.

Finally, his face registered that this was not just any horse. That he *knew* this horse.

"I *know* this horse," he said.

He walked slowly to it and touched its filthy head.

"Where did you get it?"

As Gran and Catalina explained how they'd encountered it underground during their battle with the Hollows, the Duke pulled a framed photo off the wall—the one of the carousel in front of City Hall.

He brought it to the horse before him, and then pointed to a horse in the black-and-white photo. The horse was on the outer ring, a mare rearing with its two front legs in the air. The two horses were one and the same.

"This is Gussie," the Duke said. "I haven't seen her in forty years. I can't believe it. When that carousel collapsed, we all assumed all the animals were gone. Grant, let me see your Lift again."

Gran handed him the Lift. The Duke put it onto the hoof of the wooden horse. It fit perfectly. "See? It would have gone here. Your great-great-grandfather put incredible care into something that few people would even notice. Beautifully etched brass horseshoes for carousel horses." The Duke's eyes welled up.

"Do you think you could fix her?" Catalina asked.

"You still have your tools?" Gran asked.

The Duke laughed, and pointed to the overflowing contents of the storage room. "You think I get rid of anything in a place like this?"

Chapter ONE HUNDRED AND FIVE

Lunch at the Duke's was different now. Gran and Catalina both arrived on the dot of noon, ate their lunch in five minutes, and then had the rest of the period to watch and help as the Duke restored Gussie.

There was a lot to do.

But the Duke worked with an energy that belied his age. He sanded the horse down and the dirt and grime disappeared, revealing a fresh new skin of blond wood. Gran was briefly worried that he'd have to give up his Lift to Gussie, but the Duke assured him it was more important to have the Lift on hand, not on hoof. They could make more horseshoes for Gussie, he said.

Occasionally the Duke would stop to explain how he'd originally carved a certain aspect of Gussie—her eyes, her hooves—and always the Duke was teaching them. How to use a gouge, a chisel, a carving knife. And how to refashion the lower leg of a Stargazer who had been underground for forty years. Gran knew a bit about shaping material into animals, and the Duke was impressed by his way of making something inanimate look real and look alive.

It took two weeks of lunches, but then Gussie was ready. She looked strong again.

"Nice work, Catalina. Good job, Grant," the Duke said.

"Thanks," Gran said. "But, um . . ."

"What is it?" the Duke asked.

"You can just call me Gran from now on," Gran said. "That's actually my name."

"It's not Grant?" the Duke said, smiling. It was obvious he'd known all along. "I just liked having my own name for you. But I want to call you what you want to be called."

"Thanks," Gran said.

They all looked back at Gussie.

"She almost looks new," Catalina said.

"All that's left is the paint," the Duke said. "But that's far beyond my capabilities. Making a wooden horse into something alive and in glorious color—that's a job for someone else. You know anyone with skills like that?"

Gran did know someone with skills like that.

This had been part of his plan all along.

Chapter **ONE HUNDRED AND SIX**

66 **I** didn't know your mom was an artist," Catalina said.

They were pushing Gussie through town on the wheelchair, eliciting surprised looks all the way. The large man on the dirtbike, who Gran had seen just about every day for months, stopped, stared, and then fell off his bike entirely.

"You don't know anything about my mom," Gran said. "Or my dad. And I don't know anything about your family, either. I didn't even realize your great-great-grandfather started the Catalan Carousel Company."

"Who did what?" Catalina said.

"Your great-great-grandfather—"

She interrupted him. "I heard you," she said. "But that's not true. I don't have any great-anything who started any carousel company."

Gran didn't know what to say. He would have assumed she was kidding, but her face was deadly serious. And he knew that no one he'd ever met knew anything about their ancestry.

"But your last name is Catalan," Gran said. "And the factory that made carousels here was named the Catalan Carousel Company. Don't you think there's some connection?"

Now Catalina stopped pushing. She stood on the sidewalk and her brow furrowed, as if she were doing complicated calculations in her head.

Gran continued pushing Gussie up the hill.

After a few blocks, Catalina caught up.

"You could be right," she said, and continued to think—thinking so hard her eyes were almost crossed. Then, as if embarrassed to let Gran be so right about something so big (because he *was* right), she forced her face into an expression of calm and confidence.

"I doubt it, though," she said.

Chapter **ONE HUNDRED AND SEVEN**

Gran's mother's reaction to Gussie's arrival was different from the Duke's. She did not look happy. Maybe she simply wasn't excited to see her old wheelchair carrying an enormous wooden horse. *More scuffing*, Gran assumed she was thinking.

"Mom, this is Gussie," Gran said. Then he turned around, revealing Catalina, who had been shyly standing behind him. "And this is Catalina, my best friend."

Together, Gran and Catalina explained their idea to Gran's mother—that she could restore the horse by using her painting prowess and animal-display skills.

"But this is so different! I couldn't possibly!" Gran's mother said, running her fingers over the head of Gussie. The words she said pointed to reluctance, but the tone with which she said them, and the way she touched Gussie's head—she touched her wooden mane the way she ran her hand over Maisie's sleeping head—all this said she was intrigued.

"I wouldn't even know what kind of paint to use," she said, and now her eyes were running over the horse, making calculations, plans, color schemes. Gran knew she would do it, that she couldn't possibly resist now. From the corner of his eye, he caught a smile creeping over Catalina's face. She knew too.

"I'd have to prime it," his mother said. "Then sand it down again. Then put on a base coat. Probably with a heavy paint. Something that would cover well. But what color should she be? Not white. Not gray. I'd think calico. A silver saddle. Maybe a blond mane . . ."

Chapter **ONE HUNDRED AND EIGHT**

G ran couldn't remember his mother being so busy. So inspired. She'd set up Gussie on the front porch so the paint fumes wouldn't overtake the house. By now Gran's father had fixed the porch so it no longer tilted, and had silenced the front door's squeaking. Even these small repairs had brought a new contentment to Gran's mother, and this new project, the resurrection of Gussie, sent her high onto a new plateau of constant happiness and industry.

Every day when Gran and Maisie left for school, she followed them outside, with her smock on and her box of brushes and solvents and color, and she got to work. When they returned in the afternoon, she was still there, touching up, glazing, sanding, glazing again.

In a few days, the horse looked new again, blazing with incandescent color. A few days more and Gran's mother had somehow doubled the impact—making Gussie even brighter, the details more extraordinary.

And all along, neighbors walking by stopped to see what was happening. What was a carousel horse doing on the porch of the old Flowerpetal house? And who was this woman in a wheelchair painting that horse?

As the days went by, Gran's mother met dozens of neighbors

and connected more deeply with those she'd known from the Propositions P&S phone tree. Everyone in town came to know what she was up to, and she learned the many connections all these neighbors had to the town's colorful history.

"My father used to work at the factory," said one woman, pushing a stroller with two children in it. "He did the mirrors. Such elaborate mirrors! Framed in gold, carved to look like ivy! We still have one in the garage."

"I have pictures in my house of horses like that!" an elderly man said one day. He said he'd once been the mayor of Carousel, thirty years ago. "You would have fit in with the Catalan Carousel folks like peas in a pod!"

Eventually Gran's father realized that his great-grandfather was indeed the blacksmith in charge of shoeing the horses at the Catalan Carousel Company, and he decided he would teach himself how to make horseshoes too—even if just for fun.

Gran's mother liked to work outside, and loved the frequent visits from neighbors she'd never known. Some days neighbors stayed for hours, talking of the old times, of the carousel days and of what had happened in between. Gran's mother loved to listen as she worked, as she resurrected the horse with color.

Chapter **ONE HUNDRED AND NINE**

Meanwhile, Gran's dad had found a way to get more involved in all of this, too. He was working down at the garage most days, and came home tired and with greasy hands, but he was never too tired to work an hour or so, before and after dinner, on his own Gussie-related project.

"Gussie needs a platform," he said one day while watching Gran's mother work.

And so, the next day, he'd come home from the shop with a round metal platform in the truck bed. The day after that, he brought gears, and a crank, and a motor, and soon he had his own project, and that project—to build a mini–carousel platform for Gussie—had taken over the driveway.

The days were busy for Gran and Catalina, too. During lunch and after school, and some evenings, and all weekend, they kept busy. They knew the work that needed to be done. Gussie was just the beginning.

They brought up the golden poles (after substituting other supports).

They brought up half of a zebra.
They brought up most of a cheetah.
They brought up the other half of the zebra.
And eight more horses.
And an elephant in six pieces.

And all the while, the Hollows were nowhere to be found.

"You're kidding me!" the Duke said each time Gran and Catalina brought him another animal. With sixteen creatures in his storage room, all of them needing repair but none of them beyond it, he finally threw up his hands.

"I can't believe it," he said, and then, shaking his head, he said, as if giving himself a compliment was a tough thing to admit, "Then again, they were built to last." Then he shook himself from his reverie. "But I can't restore them all. And why would we do all that anyway?"

Gran smiled. Catalina smiled.

Because that was the next part of the plan.

Chapter **ONE HUNDRED AND TEN**

And finally, one visitor in particular changed everything. Gran and Catalina were sitting with Gran's mother on the porch, and Maisie was playing in the yard, when they noticed a woman standing on the sidewalk in front of the house. The woman was very familiar-looking, but at first Gran couldn't place exactly why.

"Propositions P&S," Catalina whispered to him.

It was Phyllis Feeley. She was standing in front of Gran's house. And soon she was talking. And soon she was saying:

"That is beautiful!"

and

"I never thought Gussie could be restored to her former glory, but you did it!"

and

"What are your names?"

and

"Could you all be part of the old Flowerpetal clan?"

and

"I used to play here as a child. I grew up a block away, and knew your great-grandparents!"

and finally,

"You know how we won the battle for Propositions P&S? Well, I was thinking we could use some of the funds to restore the carousel in front of City Hall. You all wouldn't be interested in helping with such a project, would you?"

Chapter **ONE HUNDRED AND ELEVEN**

This had been Gran and Catalina's idea all along. They couldn't believe she had the same idea, too. And they couldn't believe it when, a year later, it came to be.

Or they could believe it.

They had to believe it.

Because it did. It did come to be.

The new carousel rose from the green grass in front of City Hall, and it was much like the one that had sunk forty years earlier.

It featured the work of dozens of old Catalan Carousel Factory masters like the Duke, and featured, too, the work of Gran's mother and father, and Gran, and Catalina, and a hundred more residents of Carousel who could carve and paint and build.

It had two stories.

That had been Gran's father's idea.

And it had seven speeds.

It was easily the fastest carousel ever made.

It had horses, and zebras, and a cheetah, and an elephant.

And it had Gussie, the Stargazer.

But it had new things, too. It had a capybara. It had a Komodo dragon. A narwhal.

It was beloved in the town.

It was beloved by small children, for whom a carousel was like a roller coaster.

It was appreciated by older children, who knew a carousel wasn't a roller coaster, but felt that was probably okay.

It was treasured by parents, and grandparents, and by people in other towns, and other states. People drove miles. Hundreds of miles. They walked and rode and flew and sailed to see it.

Chapter ONE HUNDRED AND TWELVE

And soon someone said, "Can you guys make another?" And soon many someones said, "Can you make another and another?"

And when the people of Carousel hesitated, the someones said, "Um, isn't that why the town is called Carousel?"

So the people of Carousel made another. Gran's father stopped fixing cars and started building carousels. And Gran's mother painted the animals, and the rest of the town got back to work, and they built another.

And another.

And another.

Chapter **ONE HUNDRED AND THIRTEEN**

A nd the Hollows?

The Hollows didn't have much to do in Carousel anymore.

"Haven't heard much from them," the Duke said. He'd just hung up the receiver from a black wall phone. "Haven't heard a peep, actually. It's as if they're in full retreat."

Gran and Catalina were in the Duke's office—his new office. He no longer ran the storage room at Carousel Middle School. Now his office was in the corner of the first floor at the Catalan Carousel Factory. That's where the president's office usually is. It wasn't far from Gran's mother's animal-painting studio, which was next to the workshop where Gran's father worked out the machinery of each carousel.

The Duke's office looked, impossibly, the same. Just like the storage room and the office of the Hemispheric Commissioner. There was the same wall of mismatched filing cabinets, and from one of the filing cabinets, the Duke retrieved three oversized sandwiches, distributed two of them to Gran and Catalina, and sat down.

"Wait!" he said, and got up, hustled to another filing cabinet, opened the middle drawer, and set the turntable spinning. He dropped the needle and the tinkle of Cuban music filtered through the room.

"I think I know what you guys did," the Duke said with his mouth full. As always, it sounded like he was talking through a pillow. "I should have figured out what you two figured out, but I didn't. So I want to thank you. Happiness above can solve the sadness below. You figured that out. And that the best way to fight the Hollows is not with hockey sticks and two-by-fours, but with . . ."

The Duke couldn't finish. He was swallowing a stubborn part of his turkey sub. He raised his finger, asking for a moment.

But there was no need to wait. Gran and Catalina knew the missing word. It was hope.

ACKNOWLEDGMENTS

The author would like to thank you for reading this book. Or skimming it till the end. Or skipping everything except these crucial last pages. Any way you got here, gratitude eternal. He'd also like to thank Katherine Harrison and everyone at Penguin Random House who worked on the book and put it out into the world. Some other people who helped bring this book to fruition include Amanda Uhle and Trixie and Frank Uhle, Andrew Wylie, Luke Ingram, Terry and Eric Fan (who did the beautiful cover), Em-J Staples, Flip Kimball and the Kimball family, Lucie Putnam, Ajani DeFreece, Maeyana Vogt, VV, BV and AV, and especially:

AARON RENIER!

Who, as you know from the dust jacket and elsewhere in the book, did all the illustrations in this book. Would you like to hear a great story—I think it's great; you decide—about how the author and Aaron met? Well, one day Aaron was drawing pictures for kids at a place called 826CHI. This was in Chicago, and 826CHI was (and is) a place where Chicago kids can go to write stories and create their own books. And this particular day, Aaron was illustrating the work that these Chicago schoolkids had written. The author got to know Aaron that way, and they stayed in touch. About a year later, the legendary Maurice Sendak created a program where young illustrators could come to his house in Connecticut, stay in his barn (it was a barn but was very nice and not barn-like in smell) and spend a few weeks learning from the master—Sendak himself! The author recommended this program to Aaron, and Aaron was accepted and went! And he learned much. Then he returned to Chicago, and continued to draw illustrations to accompany the work written by public school students in Chicago. It was many years later that the author wrote this book, *The Lifters*, and thought Aaron would be the perfect person to illustrate it. He said yes, and worked very hard, and many late hours, and used many pencils and charcoal sticks, and got many blisters and one or two headaches. Thank you, Aaron!

ABOUT 826 NATIONAL

We just mentioned something called 826CHI, which is a nonprofit writing and tutoring center in Chicago. But there are also similar and related centers in many other cities, including San Francisco, Los Angeles, Boston, New York, Detroit, Minneapolis/St. Paul, New Orleans, Washington, D.C., London, Stockholm, Dublin, Buenos Aires, Florence, Milan, and Oakland—among so many other places. In all of these places, kids can write creatively, make books, write plays and poems, and perform their work in front of audiences. These spaces offer all programs free of charge, and all with great joy and aplomb. Please find more information at **www.826national.org** and **www.daveeggers.net.** And if you don't happen to live in or near one of these big cities, you can experience many of the lessons and writing prompts 826 National teaches by visiting this website: **www.826Digital.com.** See you there.

DAVE EGGERS is an award-winning author whose novels for adults include *The Circle*, *The Monk of Mokha*, and *Heroes of the Frontier*. His books for children include *Her Right Foot*, *This Bridge Will Not Be Gray*, and *What Can a Citizen Do?* He is the cofounder of 826 Valencia, a writing and tutoring center in San Francisco that empowers young people through the written word and that has inspired similar centers all over the world. In 2018, Eggers cofounded the International Congress of Youth Voices, an annual gathering of one hundred extraordinary young writers and activists.

AARON RENIER is a cartoonist whose graphic novels include *Spiral-Bound*, *The Unsinkable Walker Bean*, and *The Unsinkable Walker Bean and the Knights of the Waxing Moon*. In 2006, he won the Eisner Award for Talent Deserving of Wider Recognition and was an inaugural recipient of a Sendak Fellowship in 2010. He lives in Chicago, where he teaches comics and drawing.